TWISTED FATE

AMY K. MCCLUNG

HOT TREE PUBLISHING

For information, contact the publisher, Hot Tree Publishing.
www.hottreepublishing.com
Edited by Hot Tree Editing
Cover design by Claire Smith
Book design by Inkstain Design Studio
ISBN: 978-1-925655-94-0

MORE FROM
AMY K. McCLUNG

SOUTHERN DEVOTION SERIES

For the Love of Gracie

Curves in the Road

Complicated Relationships

Twisted Fate

STAND-ALONES

A Little Spark

Across the Way

Still You

To Amanda—

The closest thing I ever had to a daughter. Since the first day I met you, I've admired your strength in dealing with everything life has thrown at you, the compassion you have toward others, and most of all, your positive outlook on life. Even when times seemed the toughest, you've always powered through. The character of Angel may not be based on your life, but her strength, loyalty, and loving heart were inspired by you.

ONE
ANGEL

"My name is Angel, and I'm an alcoholic." Those were the first words I spoke when they put me in rehab. The last three words were the hardest to admit in my lifetime. The other four were, "I have multiple sclerosis." At the age of twenty-three, it was a lot to take in. The bright side was I had some of the most supportive friends in the world. I owed them my life, literally; especially my friend and roommate Tristan. I asked him for the worst promise; I asked him to keep my secrets, and it almost caused him to lose something great in his life. The worst moment came when I shoved my pregnant childhood friend, Mary Jane, while in one of my drunken stupors. Her baby was fine, but it was an eye-opener for me.

Cameron, my friend and hero, was born with a silver spoon in his mouth but not a stuck-up attitude, which sometimes comes with the upbringing. He's the most generous person I know, and he paid for all my treatments. I'd have to work a lifetime and then some to pay him back, but I'd find a way.

"Rise and shine." Tricia the orderly came into my room switching on the light. Six o'clock on the dot. The first portion of the day consisted of showering with several other women in a communal bathroom with nothing but short walls between us for the semblance of privacy. At seven sharp, they served breakfast in the cafeteria. The menu contained gray slop they claimed was oatmeal, two rocks they called biscuits, and a piece of fruit of our choosing. I grabbed the last large red apple and passed it to the orderly in charge of slicing our fruit since we aren't allowed knives.

Breakfast time was nice because the cafeteria was co-ed. I'd made two male friends, Gus and Mike, who always saved me a seat. Gus stood six feet tall with a stocky build. He began drinking at the age of twelve to deal with his uncle's sexual abuse. Sixteen years later, at age twenty-eight, he had to get help for the first time due to a mandated court order after being found intoxicated in the park with no clothes on. Mike was slightly shorter and thin as a rail. His binge drinking started three years ago when he found his pregnant wife brutally murdered in their home. They were still newlyweds, only married a year, and were expecting their first child. While working overtime to save for the baby, someone broke into their home and surprised her. Luckily he had a sister who saw his problem escalating and helped him commit. He was thirty-three.

"Morning, Angel," Gus said, smiling up at me as I approached the table.

"Morning, Gus-Gus." I called him by the nickname I gave him after my favorite Disney character from *Cinderella*.

"Sleep okay?" Mike asked with a mouthful of oatmeal greeting me as well.

"Yes. I think that could've waited till you swallowed, though," I said giving him a sour look.

"Sorry, my manners ain't great," Mike admitted shyly. Growing up in the small town of Nolensville, Tennessee, his accent was very southern. His wife was the only woman he ever dated, and it was easy to see why. Mike was very timid when it came to talking to women. It took me about a week to get him to look me in the eyes and say hello.

Tricia stopped by the table and held her fist out in front of me, then opened her palm revealing a small paper cup of pills. "Here are your meds for the day, Angel. Are you having any pain?"

I gulped the meds down in one swish and shook my head. It was easier to shake my head than for her to hear the lie I'd spill. For the most part, my MS was under control with the meds, but the tremors in my legs were getting more severe by the day. Gritting my teeth, I stood as upright as I could without showing the true pain I felt.

After Tricia walked away, Gus put his fork down and leaned across the table to whisper, "Why did you lie to her?"

"How do you know I did?"

"I can see you cringe when you walk, Angel. Tell them you're in pain, and they'll give you something to help," Gus urged.

"I used alcohol to curb my pain before; I need to learn to cope with it instead of using drugs. My addiction was out of control, and I won't go there again."

Gus nodded. "Fair enough. If I can do anything to help, sugar, let me know. I can carry trays or lend a hand when the walking is too much."

Gus and Mike were some of the sweetest men I'd ever met who never wanted anything from me but friendship. Being in rehab was my worst nightmare until I met them. On the first day I showed up, Gus noticed the tears running down my cheeks as I tried to do something as simple as carry a tray with food on it. He took it from me and held the seat out, and I told him about what made me hurt. Two years ago, I could be described as curvy, but since the diagnosis, I'd lost weight in places I never wanted to lose it. Doctors said the meds would affect my appetite, and the disease itself would cause weight loss.

I'd been in rehab for three weeks, and I'd lost ten pounds. When I spoke about it in group, one of the girls made a snide remark about how she wished she could lose weight so easily and didn't know why I was complaining. The counselor asked her to be kinder with her words, but she wasn't the only one who acted out toward me since I'd been there. It's why I migrated to the men's side of the dining hall to mingle. Men weren't catty like women, in my experience. Even though I had two female best friends, I preferred spending time with men for the decreased drama.

"Angel," Marty, another orderly, called out, "It's your turn for the phone. You have fifteen minutes."

I dropped my fork and wiped my hands on the napkin. "See you guys in therapy." After disposing of the leftover food on my tray, I eased over to the phone booth. They were set up like old-fashion payphone booths with a semicomfy seat inside. First I tried my house; I wanted to speak to Tristan. When no one answered, I called Mary Jane to see if they were together, or if she knew where he might be. I was afraid to call his cell phone because I didn't think he'd answer the strange number. Mary Jane usually answered any number in case it was about her stepdaughter Katelyn. She didn't answer so they must've been having family time. There was one person left I could always count on having an ear to lend.

TWO
ANGEL

An unknown number was calling me, which meant it must be about the bar. "Cameron McIntosh speaking," I answered in my best ass-kissing business tone. The professional tone coming from my body was nauseating, but necessary.

"Hey, Cam," Angel said softly.

"Bitch, you made me put on my straight-man voice." In two seconds flat, I could go from distinguished to diva; though, it was a talent I flaunted proudly.

Angel laughed heartily, and it made my heart smile. The last few times I had spoken to her she'd been down in the dumps and very negative. Rehab seemed to be working wonders for her.

"I need a pick-me-up. I had a rough night and would like a little

Cam-wow." Being the comic relief was what I did best. Since high school, Gracie, Mary Jane, and Angel had been my tight-knit group of friends. In the last couple of years, we'd added significant others to the mix and grown into a large family unit. One thing was unchanged; they still leaned on me when times were roughest.

"You came to the right place, chica. If you were a man, I could Cam-wow you to the moon and back even over the phone." I lowered my voice and asked in a sensual voice, "What are you wearing?"

Angel started to cry. Not the reaction I was going for in the moment. "I miss you so much. I miss everyone. I don't know if I'm strong enough to get better. I'm so ashamed of everything I put you guys through, especially Tristan and Mary Jane." Angel had never displayed her emotions so openly with us until recently. Most of the time, she acted as though she hadn't a care in the world, which was the reason most of us missed her problem for so long. Since the day she revealed her alcoholism, she'd opened up about her life more freely.

I needed to put on my serious tone again. "I know I'm over the top most of the time. Expressing myself in silly ways and being over emotional at times are the ways I deal with my pain. We all have pain, and we all have ways to mask it. Silliness is *my* way to cover my emotional turmoil. *Yours* was alcohol to cover your physical pain. Do you know why I fell in love with Gavin? He saw through the act. He called 'bullshit' I guess you could say."

Angel laughed and said, "I've called bullshit on you many

times, Cam."

"Touché."

"One day I want to hear more about you and Gavin. For now, I have to get off the phone. I love you, Cam." Angel was the best at hiding her pain in our group. As close as our group of friends were, sometimes we focused too much on having fun and missed signs of trouble. In a way, I felt like I'd let both Angel and Gracie down by not saving them fast enough.

"Love you too, bitch. Sweet dreams, Angel girl."

I hung up the phone and flopped myself down in my comfortable recliner. The soft grey material mimicked the arms of a big squishy teddy bear. When Gavin's away, it was my version of comfort food. Thanksgiving was the next week. Gavin, my husband, negotiated commercial real estate for a living and was out of town working on a sale. After I finished my workday, I spent the evening with my baby girl, Addison Grace.

Living as a married gay male was not easy in Tennessee, a place where there was a church every few miles. My sex life defined me in my home state. For instance, when I took new jobs, I had to explain to my boss that I was married to a man. It's not a requirement, but it made things less complicated in the end if you put it out there right away. Luckily in my line of work, interior design, people automatically assumed if you're a male designer, then you're gay.

For me, it's a valid assumption, but I knew many straight men in the business as well. Although I was positive straight men didn't walk into their boss's office and say, "Hey, man, just thought I should let you know I like sleeping with blonde women." Yet somehow, my love of penis over vagina was a vital part of who I was according to too many people.

Gavin was my saving grace, which reminded me of my other saving grace, my best friend Gracie. Without those two people in my life, many days I'd want to give up. I put on a happy persona, a flamboyant stereotypical gay character to hide the pain I felt. Before I came out in high school, I tried to "butch it up" by playing sports and going camping, even trying to date a girl or two. Nothing felt right. Even Gracie, the most beautiful woman I knew, wasn't someone I was attracted to, yet Heath Ledger… look out! There were ten things I wanted to do to him, no "Joker" about it, and man what a tail on that knight! I'm off topic; sexy guys tended to do that to me. And lord help anyone who mentioned John Bender in front of me because they're in for hours of gushing.

Mary Jane offered to be our surrogate and carried Addison after our grueling battle with adoption agencies. Even though gay marriage was recognized as legal, the state we lived in didn't always agree with the decision, making it difficult to be recognized as legally married, which was one of the qualifications to adopt with some agencies in the state. With the controversy surrounding gay marriage, even a year after the legalization, we were beyond grateful for Mary Jane's offer.

Mary Jane was our lifesaver. Addison was the best thing that ever happened to Gavin and me, besides each other of course.

My angel child let out a wail from her bedroom. Her wailing cry got me running quick. I hated to hear my baby girl upset.

"Hey, sugar-booger, Daddy's here," I said as I lifted her from her bed.

Snot bubbled from her nostril and her body shook with deep breaths from the passing sobs. It broke my heart. While rubbing her back, I kissed the blonde curls on her sweet head. She glanced up looking around. At eighteen months old, she was very intuitive.

"Da-Ga?" she asked confused.

She was asking for Daddy Gavin. She called me Da-Ca, and it sounded the same as Da-Ga, but we liked to pretend she was making the distinction. Every parent knew their kid was the smartest ever; Gavin and I were no exception. "Daddy Gavin is out of town, beautiful girl. I miss him too." I made silly noises and planted kisses all over her cheeks until she began giggling. "Daddy likes the sound of you laughing much better."

I carried her to my room to lie down for the evening. When Gavin wasn't around, it was lonely for both of us, so we stuck together. Placing pillows along one side of the bed, on the floor, and at the end of the bed as well, I set her down. She's a roller when she slept so the more cushions keeping her from hitting the floor the better. And I was known to be an overprotective dad. We went through a lot, and Mary Jane made so many sacrifices, I wasn't going to let this one so much as scrape her knee on my watch.

My phone rang again. I was very popular, what could I say. "Hello, gorgeous."

The number on my caller ID showed Mary Jane, but the voice coming through the phone was her husband, Derrick. "Hello yourself, sexy."

"I know you're trying to be funny, but it's too true to laugh at. What's up, Big D? Scratch that nickname, too graphic and awkward," I said thinking about Joe Manganiello in *Magic Mike* as Big Dick Richie.

Derrick chuckled and said, "MJ is on bed rest for the remainder of her pregnancy and Katelyn is sick. I think she has the flu. I need to get her to the doctor and possibly drop her off with my mom for a few days. Is there any way you can open the club? Marcus will be there in a few hours to run things for us."

Glancing over at Addison sleeping peacefully, I groaned. "I would run down there in a second for you, if I could. Gavin's still out of town, and I have a little girl having night terrors. She just got back to sleep."

"Shit. I hoped Gav was back. I'll check with Ashton."

After hanging up the phone with Derrick, I curled up next to my daughter and drifted off to sleep.

THREE

ANGEL

My legs buckled underneath me as I tried to get out of bed one morning. I didn't have the strength to pick myself up; my arms wouldn't cooperate. Lying on the floor, I stared up at the ceiling and gave in to defeat. My eyes stung with tears trying to break free for the physical and emotional pain I was experiencing.

I was twenty-three years old, sprawled out on the floor of a hospital room suffering from a potentially debilitating disease a day before Thanksgiving. *What happened to my life?* Even though the moment felt like the lowest possible time ever, I wouldn't allow myself to cry. I fought the tears until my head hurt from concentrating.

Tricia opened the door and said, "Angel, rise and—" She spotted me on the floor and dropped her clipboard as she fell to her knees next to me. "Are you hurt?"

"I'm having a bad day. Can you help me up?"

Tricia placed her arm around my shoulder, helping me upright, and then lifted me up onto the bed. My body ached as she dropped me to the mattress. I cringed in pain and held back the tears once more. "Do you need some pain medicine? I can call the doctor and—"

"No. A little suffering will do me good."

Tricia sat next to me and sighed heavily. "You're too hard on yourself, Angel. You've met people here, and most of them are here because of a court order. You checked in on your own."

"Not really. My friends had an intervention and convinced me to check in," I corrected her.

Tricia rolled her eyes. "Please. Do you have any idea how many of those interventions take place every day and how many actually work? It's a high number of interventions and a very low percentage of success. Your strength got you here. You don't have to be that person anymore, the one who drinks to disguise their pain or holds back tears to hide their hurt. You need to heal and you need to forgive yourself for your mistakes. I've been watching you since you got here, and trust me, you're a success story."

Tricia patted my hand softly. "Lie down. I'll tell the doctor you don't feel well, and come back to check on you in an hour. I'll bring you a plate of food too." She paused before leaving and turned one last time to ask, "Do you need me to help you to the bathroom before I go? I should've asked that first I suppose."

I chuckled. "Yeah, that's probably a good idea." After helping me to the restroom and back, she left me to finish her rounds.

Tricia brought breakfast as promised, but my appetite wasn't there so the food remained on my nightstand table as I rested in the bed. After a few hours, my door opened and shut quickly. I opened my eyes to see Gus standing there looking frantic.

"Gus-Gus, what's up?"

He peered through the small window of my room looking for orderlies. "I'm not supposed to be in here, but Mike and I were worried about you. I volunteered to check in. Mike's too skittish. I'm stealthier than he is too, somehow."

"I'm good, Gus-Gus." I chuckled a little at his confusion over the fact someone his size was easier to miss than someone like Mike who was practically invisible when turned sideways.

Gus's gaze moved to the clump of oatmeal and plate containing dry toast and a banana. "You haven't eaten a bite of breakfast and it's almost lunchtime."

My stomach turned at the thought of food. "You just want to watch me eat a banana, you old perv."

Gus guffawed and then covered his mouth quickly hoping no one heard him. "Get better, sugar. We missed you this morning." He leaned over and planted a gentle kiss on my forehead.

"It'll pass, it always does. Go keep Mike company. I know you guys fall apart without me there."

Gus grinned and shook his head before walking out the door. Gus was cute in his own way. He kept his hair cut short and his beard scruffy. He showed me a picture from a few years before when he had a porn-stache and I begged him to never make that mistake again. His stocky build made him appear a bit threatening, but he was a big fluffy teddy bear. When my rehabilitation was complete, I planned to help him find a good woman.

Tricia came back to check on me an hour later. As soon as her eyes landed on my uneaten food, her hand went to her hip and her foot tapped the floor in annoyance. "You have to keep up your strength, Angel."

"I'm not hungry. I can't force myself to eat. Tomorrow's Thanksgiving, aren't we having a big feast? I'll eat then."

Tricia exhaled, deep and loud. "Fine. I came in here to see if you were up to getting out of this room for lunch. I'll let you rest some more. I'm leaving the banana though in case you change your mind. And you missed the announcement. Everyone gets a fifteen-minute Skype session with their family tomorrow. There was a signup sheet. You were signed up for four. I hope that's all right. Gus signed your name."

"It's perfect." It would be perfect if I had family to call. My parents and I hadn't spoken in a year. When I moved home from Florida, I ignored their calls because I was too busy to talk, or too drunk;

eventually, they stopped calling. My mother left a message letting me know she loved me but couldn't keep reaching out to someone who wouldn't reach back. And my friends, well, I was sure I'd ruined things with them. At least I knew Cameron would speak to me if no one else would.

FOUR

CAMERON

Gracie and Ashton hosted Thanksgiving dinner this year. Gavin and I promised to take it the following year. The very pregnant Mary Jane sat at the dining room table filling eggs with the deviled egg mixture. They gave her the easiest job possible since she'd been told to stay off her feet.

Gracie grabbed Gavin straight away to help Ashton and Derrick in the kitchen. She dragged me, with Addison in hand, to her bedroom to keep watch on her and Autumn, Gracie and Ashton's daughter, until dinner. Macy, Tristan's little sister, would take over babysitting duties for me after dinner.

While I was watching the little divas in training, Tristan showed up with his new girlfriend, Lanie. Also, Marcus, one of the bartenders from A Shot in the Dark, came in with his date Bailey. It seemed Bailey and Tristan had a fling before he met Lanie, and the two women got into a bit of a catfight. I hated I missed the whole thing.

The women came to an understanding, and dinner went off without a hitch. The food was good, and the company was even better. Ashton carved the turkey, and the rest of the food was passed around the table until our plates were filled to the brim.

Tristan stood up and tapped a fork against his glass. "Ashton, Gracie, I want to thank you for including Macy, Lanie, and me in your family dinner today. I'm very thankful for everyone at this table, in fact. Since the day Macy and I moved here, you guys have been the family we always wanted. I think I speak for Macy too when I say we love you. Though we are missing one of our members, this feels like a perfect day. Happy Thanksgiving." He ended the toast by holding up a glass.

It was my turn to say something. "I have a surprise. Gracie, can I use your laptop?" Gracie grabbed her laptop from her bedroom and brought it to the table. I checked my watch and then urged, "Ooh, sign in, please. We only have about a minute." Gracie logged in, and I couldn't hide my grin when a ringtone sounded. With a push of a few buttons, I greeted the face on the screen, "Hello, beautiful."

Lifting the laptop, I turned it to face everyone, and they saw Angel smiling back at them. "Happy Thanksgiving!" she exclaimed with a wave. Everyone cheered and returned the sentiment. "For the holiday, they allowed us to Skype our families. I only have ten more minutes, but it's so good to see you all." She choked back tears.

As Gracie and Mary Jane dominated Angel's attention for a moment, I noticed Marcus and Tristan whispering to each other. I hoped it wasn't more drama with the chick Marcus brought. Whatever it was, they ended it quickly. Tristan leaned forward and said, "You are very much missed today, Angel. In your honor though, I'm eating a plate for you."

Angel chuckled softly. "Thanks so much, T. That means the world to me." She rolled her eyes playfully. "Only one week to go and I'll be home with all of you. I only have about two minutes left now. Is Macy there?"

I had noticed Macy left the room when Angel came on screen but didn't ask questions because Tristan hadn't been fazed by it. I supposed because he didn't see her. She'd grown close to Angel since they moved to town, and I knew seeing her in rehab must be hard for her. Macy was one of the smartest teenagers I'd ever known, but as big as her brain was, her heart was even bigger.

"I'll go get her real quick," Tristan said.

"So, Angel, any hot men in there?" The minute the question came out of my mouth, Gavin smacked my arm playfully and everyone else laughed. "What? I've seen *28 Days*, Angel could meet her Viggo Mortensen in there."

Seeing a grin light up Angel's face was all I wanted to achieve with the question, and it worked. "No Viggo, sorry, Cam. But I do have two great guys in here looking out for me. They've been my rocks. When we get out, I'd love for them to meet all of you."

Tristan was gone for too long, and he came back without Macy. "Sorry, Angel, Macy's in the restroom. She said to tell you she loves you and can't wait for you to come home."

Angel gave a teary wave goodbye and blew a few kisses our way before the screen went black.

Gracie wiped tears from her eyes, and Ashton placed his hand over hers. I turned my attention to Mary Jane who was also wiping her eyes. "Look here, bitches... oops... Sorry, I forgot there are children present. Look here, babes, no crying today. Angel wouldn't want it, and I can't stand to see your mascara streaking. Get a grip, both of you."

"Yes, sir," Mary Jane said with a firm salute.

Gavin leaned over and kissed my cheek. "What the hell was that?" I asked before grabbing him and pulling him into a lip-lock, which elicited a cheer from the others. "That's better. None of that cheek kissing with my man."

Gavin seemed uncomfortable, which set off warning bells in my head. Kissing in front of our friends had never been an issue; we always knew they'd never judge us. Neither of us went for public displays of affection because of how some people would react when they saw two men kiss. We preferred to shield ourselves from any commentary. Neither of us was ashamed of who we were, but no matter how strong you were, words did hurt. Strangers' words hurt more than those of loved ones because they didn't hold back to spare your feelings. Grabbing his empty plate, he stalked away toward the kitchen. I lifted my napkin from my lap and placed it on the table. "Excuse me, I'll be back."

Gavin stood with his palms on the counter and his face looking down at the floor. He didn't move when he heard me come in the room. I stepped up and embraced him from behind. With my head laying on his shoulder, I asked, "What's wrong, baby?"

Gavin placed his hands against mine on his chest. "It's nothing."

"I know you better than anyone. It's not nothing. You've been a bit distant since you came home from your trip. Did something happen?" Since I always played the strong one in our group of friends, Gavin took on the responsibility in our relationship. Whenever I was lost, he was the voice of wisdom.

"I lost the deal." Negotiating commercial real estate deals was Gavin's job. He was the southeast representative for his company, which was how we obtained such an amazing deal on A Shot in the Dark when we found our locale.

"Okay, babe. I know it sucks, but you've lost deals before."

Gavin pulled away and turned to face me. "I lost the deal because of this," he said holding up his left hand displaying his wedding ring.

"Because you're married?" I asked, completely confused at where this conversation was going. "Was he hitting on you?"

Gavin chuckled sardonically. "Because I'm married to a man. The last thing he wanted to do was hit on me." Not sure why I had been so dense, we'd dealt with bigotry so much in life because of who we loved.

"What the fuck? Tell me what happened, I'm lost." Between the two of us, I was the drama queen who became paranoid about odd occurrences. Rationality was Gavin's forte, and I couldn't understand his behavior.

"I arrived a little early to the meeting. We were exchanging small talk, and the buyer asked me how long I'd been married. I told him we'd been married for three years. He asked about children so of course I talked about Addison. I missed her and used the opportunity to take out my phone and look at her picture." Pressing buttons on his phone, he slid the screen open to show me the picture. "My favorite picture of you and Addy is the background of my phone so I showed him. He asked if you were my brother. I didn't skip a beat in correcting him. He got a look on his face. You know the one we see all the time, the look of disgust instantly alerting you to a homophobe. He excused himself from the room, and five minutes later, the secretary comes in to tell me he had to leave and we'd reschedule."

"Another homophobe exposed, no need to worry," I assured him.

"As I was walking out the door I overheard him talking to his partners. He told them he was going with another firm, any firm that didn't hire faggot pedophiles. He actually assumed you and I were..." Tears formed in his eyes as he choked on the words.

My chest tightened with anger. "He assumed two men with a baby had to be molesting that baby?" Gavin nodded silently. "Fuck him. Who cares what an ignorant bigot says?" I grabbed Gavin by the shoulders forcing him to face me again. "Baby, look at me." When his eyes met mine, I wanted to scream in anger at the pain this idiot caused him.

A pang of hurt shot through my chest as a thought occurred to me. I pulled away to search Gavin's eyes for the truth of what I suspected. "You never kiss me on the cheek. A minute ago, when you did, is that because you're ashamed of me now?"

Gavin's eyes widened, and I saw my hurt mirrored in them. "What? No! I've never been ashamed of you, Cam. I love you. I don't know Marcus and Bailey or how they feel about people like us. I didn't want them to judge us."

"Who gives a damn what people think? We love each other and that's all that matters. If people don't like it, fuck them. But for future reference, Marcus and Bailey are both cool." Even if I didn't know how they felt about men kissing, I didn't give two fucks either. Marrying Gavin was the best decision I ever made, and I refused to allow people to make me feel ashamed of our love.

I pulled him into my arms and held him. The tables were turned. Normally I was the mess and Gavin brought me back. "Oh, I'm sorry," Gracie said as she walked into the room. "Something wrong?"

"We're good," I answered before Gavin could. As well as she knew me, Gracie would be able to read my face and know I wouldn't want to talk about it. She picked up on the vibe and didn't ask questions.

"Tristan had to leave. He had a family emergency with his mom. He's going to call us later to let us know."

"His mom? Isn't she in a nursing home?" Tristan raised his sister Macy when his mother's Alzheimer's worsened and his father abandoned them.

Gracie scraped the plates off into the trash and loaded the dishwasher as she answered. "Yes. The nursing home called and said she took a turn for the worse and doesn't have much time."

"Shit. What a Thanksgiving this has been."

FIVE

ANGEL

ONE YEAR LATER

"**M**y name is Angel, and today is my one-year anniversary of sobriety," I said into the microphone at my weekly AA meeting. Dozens of faces stared up at me, ranging from newly sober to people celebrating decades of sobriety. Twirling my year chip in my hand, I smiled at how far I'd come.

"Last year I spent Thanksgiving in rehab talking with my friends through Skype for a few short minutes. This year on Thanksgiving, I had so much to be thankful for. My friends accepted me back into their lives and forgave me for my actions when I was under the influence of alcohol. Rehab gave me more than sobriety. It gave me my life back and it gave me two friendships, which I will cherish for eternity. Only one of them is here with me today. Gus-Gus."

Gus walked down the aisle to me and gave me a hug at the podium. His strong embrace was the best high I could achieve without falling off the wagon. He stood by me as I continued my story. "The biggest struggle in maintaining sobriety for me is grief. I don't deal well with it on my own. Gus and I were in rehab with a man named Mike. He was a sweet southern gentleman who never hurt anyone other than himself. Two months ago, he committed suicide." Gus grabbed my hand, squeezing for support. "Gus called to tell me, and the first thing I did was pick up a bottle of Jack Daniel's at the liquor store. I cried until I couldn't cry anymore, and then I opened the bottle and poured a glass. As I took in the scent of whiskey, my old friend, I picked up my phone and dialed Gus. He came over immediately, and instead of drinking, we sat and traded stories of Mike and laughed about his thick southern accent and his goofy behavior."

I held Gus's hand up in the air. "This man is the reason I am sober today." Everyone in the room gave Gus and me a standing ovation. We embraced and cried for a few moments over our lost friend and our mutual sobriety. Mike's death had been hard on both of us. We felt we should've known he was ready to break, but deep down we knew there was nothing we could have done. After reading his suicide note, which mentioned only Gus and me, other than his wife and the child he never met, it gave us a little peace knowing we meant so much to him.

After the meeting, we went to a diner to have a cup of coffee. "To

Mike," I said holding my mug up for him to tap in toast to our friend.

"Have you begun dating yet?" Gus asked me. In rehab, we were encouraged not to engage in any relationships until we were stable in our sobriety. I've never been someone who dated. I'd go out, get drunk, and go home with a different guy every weekend, sometimes twice a week. Going back to that lifestyle was no longer an option or a desire of mine.

"No. Sadly I don't know how to date."

Gus laughed at what he thought was me making a joke. His chuckle trailed off as he noted my serious expression. "You're one of the sexiest women I've ever met. I know you've been on a date."

I leaned over and gave him a kiss on the cheek. "You're a sweet man, Gus. I've got a lot of demons in my past. I never told you this. It's something I never told anyone until a few years ago. My first experience with sex was rape." No one knew this about me until recently. When Gracie revealed her rape to me, I felt it was only right to confide in her my understanding with my own experience. "I went on a date my junior year of high school, and the guy wouldn't take no for an answer. I thought I was being strong by not letting it turn me into a sniveling mess. Two days later, I went out with another guy and slept with him. I cried afterwards for a bit, and then again, I told myself I wouldn't let it break me. So I never let myself have feelings for anyone. I've had sex with a lot of men. I'm not proud of the numbers, but I'm not a prude either. I want things to be different. I'd like to be romanced, wined and dined. I need to be wooed by someone at least once. When I couldn't heal myself by being with other men, I turned to alcohol."

Gus moved from his side of the booth and took the seat next to me. He wrapped his arm around my shoulder and pulled me close. "You're even more amazing than I knew."

I couldn't hold back the laughter at his absurd statement. "How can you be proud of me for sleeping around?"

"I'm proud of you for knowing your limits. You deserve to be wooed and romanced. If you weren't my best friend in this entire world, I'd be the first in line for the honor." Gus's complimentary support made my heart flutter. Not many men had said something so sweet to me without wanting to get in my pants.

"Thank you. My question is, where do we find dates? We can't exactly go to a club or bar. Is the Internet our only option?" Meeting someone online wasn't the worst option I could imagine, but it opened up a higher chance of meeting someone dishonest.

Gus pondered the question a moment with his index finger against his lips and his eyes focused upward. "I think our only option is a meet-cute at the supermarket."

"Are you going to hang out in produce and ask women about their melons?" I teased.

"It could work." Throwing me a wink, Gus leaned his head against mine.

After paying the bill, we went back to Gus's place and stayed up all night talking about our options for the future.

SIX

CAMERON

A Shot in the Dark was empty when I arrived. Derrick asked me to open for the night. Gavin took Addison to his mom Maria's house for dinner. Gavin's biological parents were Christian extremists. They'd spat hate at him since the day he revealed he was into guys. They even kicked him out of their house the same day with nowhere to go. Ashton Collins was dating Gavin's sister, Addie, at the time, and the Collinses became the surrogate family he always wanted. Since the day they took him in, he'd considered Ashton's and Derrick's parents his own.

Their father passed away almost three years ago when he was killed by a drunk driver. When they opened A Shot in the Dark, they swore they'd take every precaution to not send drunk drivers out to kill other loved ones. And so far, our sober ride program had worked quite well. It cut into the profits a little, but we all believed it was well worth it.

Someone entered the door to the club, and I tensed up wondering who was here so early. "Hello?"

Marcus popped his head into the office and waved. "Hey, boss man. I'm early, I know. My car is in the shop so my buddy had to drop me off. You don't mind if I hang out, do you?"

"Shit, of course not. As long as you hang out in here and keep me company. It gets creepy when this place is empty." Marcus flopped down on the leather couch across the room. "Careful on that couch, I'm pretty sure Ashton and Gracie and Mary Jane and Derrick use it to do the nasty."

Marcus grinned mischievously. "I've used it at least once myself." Sliding his hand along the top of the leather, his smirk grew wider as he appeared lost in a memory.

I scoffed. "You're a sick bastard. Who with?"

Marcus laughed. "I thought I was a sick bastard?"

"You are, but so am I, and I want details. Go."

"Bailey. We took a tangle on this couch a couple of times last year when I was covering the holiday shifts." Momentarily his eyes shifted downward, and I saw what appeared to be regret wash across his features.

"Are you two a thing now?" Perhaps his sadness was over unrequited love for this woman. Sometimes I couldn't help being a romantic.

"Bailey doesn't have relationships with people. She sleeps with them and moves on. It's ancient history now. She's a cool chick though, no hard feelings there." Marcus placed his arms behind his head and got comfortable by propping his feet up on the other end of the couch. "I haven't been with anyone in three months now."

The sip of coffee I'd taken came spewing forth in response to his comment. "Has your dick fallen off?" Three months without sex might as well have been a lifetime to me. Oh, I'd gone without it, but not by choice.

Marcus guffawed. "It's pretty dark blue at this moment, but it's still there."

"We need to get you laid, Marcus. Your hot Italian body should be appreciated." Marcus had a beautiful olive tone to his skin, and his body looked average until you saw him flex his muscles. Each time he lifted a box of liquor for the bar the guns came out and the ladies swooned. I'd swooned a little myself. It was odd for him to go so long without sex. He was one of the biggest players I knew.

"I've had enough sex to last a lifetime. Don't get me wrong, I'm not signing up for the monastery, but I'm slowing things down."

There had to be more that led to his behavior.

"For what reason?" Befuddled barely touched how I felt at hearing these words. In the few years I'd known Marcus, I never imagined him saying them.

"Have I ever told you about my friend Calvin?" Answering with a shake of my head, he continued. "We've been friends since we were three. At the age of thirteen, we decided girls weren't so icky. By fifteen, we'd both lost our virginity and learned how to sweet talk the ladies."

"I'm not sure I ever got over thinking girls were icky." I winked at him.

Laughing, Marcus continued his story. "Calvin makes me look like a monk in comparison to the number of ladies we've been with. Age sixteen Marcus would be proud of the number, but twenty-five-year-old Marcus is not as thrilled about these conquests. For years, we worked as the other's wingman until recently. Calvin called me up about three months ago—"

"Shit," I exclaimed as I opened the book in front of me, momentarily interrupting his story.

Marcus sat straight up. "What's wrong, Cam?"

"Tristan left his plane tickets here and he leaves in the morning. He and Lanie are going to Vegas for their honeymoon." I dialed Tristan and he picked up on the second ring. "Hey, man, your tickets are in the office. You might want to swing by and get them."

"Damn," Tristan replied. "I'm at Derrick and MJ's house. I've got Craig and Katelyn here. Derrick will be with you shortly, and Lanie is out with the girls. Maybe I can call her and see if she'd swing by to get them." Craig and Katelyn were Mary Jane and Derrick's children, so Tristan couldn't leave them alone, and I was sure he didn't want to drag them out to the bar.

"Hang on," I held the phone away from my mouth and asked, "Marcus, do you mind running an errand for me? On the clock."

"Did you forget I don't have a car.?"

"Shit. Everyone is so high maintenance right now," I whined. "Fine, you can drive my car." Returning my attention to the phone, I said, "No worries, T. I'm sending Marcus your way."

"Thanks, man, you're the best."

"Best friend, best husband, best ass, yep that's me." I could practically hear Tristan rolling his eyes as he laughed before hanging up the phone.

SEVEN

ANGEL

Gracie, Mary Jane, Lanie, and I spent the evening celebrating Lanie's last few hours as a "single woman." She married Tristan the past summer at the bar, but none of us could work out bachelor and bachelorette parties to fit everyone's schedule. Instead, we decided to have their parties just before the honeymoon. With Macy away at college, and the bar fully staffed, Lanie and Tristan decided to fly out to Vegas for a week. The girls were accommodating my addiction by having dinner at a restaurant instead of dancing their night away at a club while drinking and doing crazy stuff like wearing penises on a headband.

The waiter came by to fill our drink orders. "Is it ladies' night tonight? I know a group of ladies as beautiful as all of you cannot be single." Awkward moment number one as I sat at the table as the one single lady. Mary Jane offered me a sympathetic look, and I wanted to scream. I despised being pitied.

"I'm getting married tomorrow," Lanie answered with a sickeningly happy smile. She'd been married for a few months, but it was fun to pretend.

"Congratulations! What can I get from the bar for your celebration?" Awkward moment number two as everyone shifted uncomfortably and glanced in my direction before telling him they weren't drinking tonight. "What? That's inexcusable! A bachelorette night without margaritas or cosmos is a sin. So, cough up those orders."

"It's fine, girls. Order a drink. I'll be the designated driver." It was easier to cop to that excuse than to explain to a perfect stranger about being an alcoholic and that my friends were attempting to be supportive. I appreciated the gesture, I did. Instead of feeling supported, it was suffocating me. I'd held them back from living life because of my mistakes, and I wouldn't do it anymore.

"No really, sweet tea is fine for me. Thanks." Lanie smiled as she said the words, but disappointment rolled across her features.

I sighed in defeat. When the waiter left, I stood up. "I'm going to take off. I have a headache and… No, I'm not going to lie. I'm very uncomfortable and you are too. I appreciate you all including me tonight, but I want you to have fun. So, order a drink from the bar, stop by the Hustler and pick up some penis headbands and go have a blast at A Shot in the Dark."

Lanie jumped up and threw her arms around my neck. "Thanks for being here, Angel. Why don't you go over to Mary Jane's and keep Tristan company with Craig and Katelyn? I'm sure he'd love another adult there and would be especially happy if it was you."

Lanie's idea sounded like the best night to me. I didn't bother calling him. I drove straight over and knocked on the door. Greeted with a look of surprise I watched as he poked his head outside to glance around for other surprises. "Where are the rest of the girls?"

"They're going to A Shot in the Dark." He appeared taken aback and a bit disgusted probably assuming they ditched me. I clarified. "I told them to go. They need to feel comfortable drinking without worrying about the alcoholic elephant in the room. I didn't think you'd mind my company."

"Of course not," he said wrapping his arm around my shoulder and pulling me inside. "Craig's asleep and Katelyn's watching *Frozen* for the…. I've lost count of how many times the kid has seen that movie."

We passed the living room where Katelyn was deeply enthralled in her movie and took a seat in the kitchen. Tristan poured me a virgin Rum and Coke before sitting down across from me. "Did you have any fun tonight?" he asked. "When you showed up alone I didn't know what to think. I know those women are not the kind to exclude someone, especially you."

"Yeah, of course, I love those girls. I know they could have fun without drinking, but they need to feel free to do what they want. Tell me about your bachelor party the other night."

Tristan groaned. "Cameron hired a stripper thinking it would be a great idea. Have you ever seen the episode of *Friends* where Phoebe is getting married and they hire a stripper played by Danny DeVito?"

I snorted at the image of the scene in my head. "It's one of my favorite episodes." I gasped. "Did he get you a Danny DeVito stripper?"

Tristan shook his head and chuckled. "I wish. The woman was attractive, but her dance moves were like something I can't even describe. It was awkward and uncomfortable. Strippers have never been my thing though. Other than that, we had a great time."

We sat in silence for a moment, I felt Tristan's gaze on me.

"What's wrong, Angel?"

Before I could answer, Craig's crying rang out from the bedroom and the doorbell rang at the same time. "Can you get the door for me? It should be Marcus from the club. I'll be back."

Tristan sprinted toward the back of the house. I opened the front door to see an olive-skinned, black-haired stranger standing on the front porch. His eyes moved over my body sending shivers across my skin. I bit my lip as I checked him out too. "Marcus?" I asked curiously. "I'm Angel."

"Yes, you are," he murmured as he gave me another once over.

"Wow. That was a cheesy line." Even so, I found myself immensely attracted to this man.

"I apologize. I'm not a cheesy-line kind of guy. Let me start over. I'm Marcus. I work with Tristan at the bar." He paused briefly, and then said, "I know you from somewhere. Were you at their Thanksgiving dinner last year?"

It occurred to me where I remembered him from, I'd seen him in the video Skyping session we'd had while I was in rehab. I didn't want to go into such personal details of my life with a stranger on my friend's porch. "I've been to the bar before, you probably saw me there. Tristan's taking care of Craig. Can I help you with something? He didn't have a chance to tell me what you were here for."

Marcus held up two plane tickets. "He left his tickets in the office. Cameron had me drive them over so they wouldn't miss their flight tomorrow."

I took them from his hand and thanked him. "Do you want to come in for a moment and wait on Tristan?"

Marcus moved past me and went to the living room. "Hey Katie-boo," he called out. Katelyn jumped up and ran over to him exclaiming, "Uncle Marcus!"

I stood at the doorway watching their exchange. After lifting her into a big bear hug, he placed her back where she'd been sitting. He had taken a seat beside her on the couch, and she showed him some of her drawings. Compliments poured from him about what an amazing artist she was. I thought it was all puff until I walked over and saw them myself. She certainly was a talented artist. His rapport with her was endearing to see. In many ways, he reminded me of Tristan or Ashton or Derrick with their natural-born fatherly ways. The trait was incredibly sexy to witness.

"Katelyn, oh my gosh, I had no idea how artistic you were." She had drawn pictures of Anna and Elsa from the movie she'd been watching.

Katelyn shrugged. "Dad says I'm almost a better artist than Uncle Ash."

"Well, I have to agree with him." Her attention had been taken by the movie once more so Marcus and I excused ourselves from the room and went to sit in the kitchen.

"Would you like a drink?" Opening the cabinet, I stood poised to grab a glass from the shelf.

"I'm working tonight and I have to drive back in a minute," he responded.

"And a Coke would give you a sugar high and make working and driving chaotic?" I replied sarcastically.

"Sorry, I thought you were offering alcohol. A Coke would be great."

After handing him a glass with ice and a can of Coke, I suspected he knew more about me than he let on. "Why would you automatically assume I was offering you alcohol?" There was a bit more anger in my voice than I intended. *Dial it back a bit, Angel.*

"I meant no offense by it. I'm a bartender, alcohol surrounds my life."

Naturally, I'd be attracted to someone whose life revolved around alcohol. His beautiful complexion and bulging biceps would be for my viewing pleasure only. I couldn't allow myself to get involved with him. Even if his silky black hair begged my fingers to run through it while he pleasured me with his mouth. I shook my head to erase the naughty images running through my mind.

Marcus placed his hand on my arm and asked, "Are you okay?" His touch was electric as it sent shockwaves up my arm. I bit my lip to suppress a moan. I watched his lips speak to me, but didn't hear the words. I wasn't sure why this attraction to him was so strong. Perhaps it was the mention of my one true love, alcohol, seducing me into submission.

I pulled my arm away from his touch. "You should probably get back to bar. It's getting late and the crowd will be growing."

Marcus stood up. "You're right. Thanks for the drink. It's been a pleasure."

EIGHT

CAMERON

I was leaving the club at four in the morning, more than ready to get home. While Tristan was out of town, I was taking on more of the closing responsibility. Thankfully, this was the last night I had to cover him. As I approached my car, I spotted a couple of guys who had been kicked out of the bar earlier for being rowdy. I turned to go back inside and wait for Marcus when one of them approached me. "Hey, man. You're one of the owners of the club, right?" I attempted to ignore them and picked up my pace. "Hey, you have a swish in your walk. You're the faggot owner, aren't you? You like being fucked in the ass?" Laughter erupted from the rest of the group.

Fear gripped my chest as images of Gavin and Addison entered my mind. My only thought I had was to get home to see my husband and little girl. They wouldn't break me tonight. I took off in a run and was only a foot from the door when I was hit in the back of the head. I was rolled over and the next hit caught me square in the jaw. Ignoring the pain in my face, I shoved him away from me and tried to crawl back to my feet. My legs were grabbed, and I was dragged across the concrete, ripping my shirt in the process. Grooves in the pavement scraped against my bare skin. The sounds of a belt buckle being undone, and laughter surrounded me. "I can show you what a real man feels like instead of the pansy shit you're used to." As he whispered this trash in my ear, I begged for the moment to end quickly.

"Get the fuck off him!" I heard Marcus scream and the next sound was a gun being cocked. "Get out of here now before I use this thing. The safety is off and I'm a better shooter than Rick Grimes and not as willing to give second chances." The reference of the character from *The Walking Dead* must have convinced them, or it was his stern voice and the gun aimed at them. Either way, the men scurried off and Marcus bent down to help me up. "Shit, Cam. Let's take you to the hospital." Slipping his arm beneath my armpit, he pulled me up to my feet.

"No. Take me back inside for now." He helped me sit down on the couch in my office, and then I eased my head back against the soft leather. One friend I knew could fix anything and keep a secret, so I sent her a text. "If you need to go home, you can. I'll wait here for my friend."

"I'll stay," Marcus insisted.

"Earlier you had been telling me about your friend Calvin? I believe you said he called you and everything changed. What was the call about?" Distraction was the best medicine for me. My side ached and my chest and back burned; I needed to take my mind off all of it.

Marcus settled onto the couch next to me, propping his feet up on the table. "Right. Well, roughly three months ago he calls me up. We hadn't spoken for over two years before that day. He had moved to New York to pursue a career on Broadway, and it wasn't going well. After trying for months to the point of almost bankrupting himself, he got a job as a waiter at a fancy restaurant in the city. Serving businessmen and lonely rich women became his life. He called me a few times to tell me about his latest conquests. Many one-night stands with wealthy women who tipped him outrageous amounts. In a way, he'd become a gigolo. It wasn't as though he was taking money for sex, but he might as well have been. When I stopped hearing from him, I assumed it was due to his hectic lifestyle."

"What was really going on?"

"He'd been sick. The call was to tell me how bad things had become since he'd been diagnosed." Before Marcus could finish, there was a knock on the outside door. Leaving me on the couch, he opened the door to find Angel standing there. "We meet again."

Angel didn't speak. She pushed past Marcus to come to me. "Jesus, what happened?" Cringing I shifted my weight on the couch as she started pulling up my shirt checking for damage.

"A bunch of homophobes outside the club, trying to prove their manhood is bigger than mine." I chuckled to keep myself from crying instead. "I need you to cover this bruise on my face so Gavin can't see it. I don't want him to worry."

Marcus eyed Angel curiously. "Are you a makeup artist or something?"

She shook her head. "Or something. I've had enough abuse from men in my life that I know how to hide the bruises. Cameron is the only one who knows how good I am at this. I never told any of our other friends, and I hope you are trustworthy enough to keep this between us as well."

Marcus used his index finger and made a cross over his chest. "Your secret is safe with me." Probably sensing we needed a moment alone, he said, "I'm going to look at the security footage in Ash's office and see if I can get a good picture of the guys. We can tell the others they damaged some customer cars or something."

"Thanks, Marcus." With a nod of his head, he left the room, closing the door behind him.

"You need to lie down. I'll text Gavin from your phone and let him know you're doing paperwork for a few hours and you'll be home soon." Angel took Marcus's place next to me with her head next to mine.

"Tell me what happened, Cam."

"It was a typical homophobic attack, Angel. The guys were in here drinking, and we kicked them out for acting like assholes. They're regulars. I've seen them all before. I guess they've seen me with Gavin because they knew I was gay. They called out to me and I tried to run, but I didn't get far before they caught me." I sat up and cleared my throat from the emotions bubbling up. "You can guess the rest."

"We need to take some pictures of your injuries in case you decide to press charges."

"No. I don't want Gavin to know anything about it." Gavin doesn't snoop, we trust each other, but if by accident those photos came up on my phone I'd have to tell him about what happened. All I wanted was to protect my family from more heartache.

"We'll take them on my phone. And I'll delete them later if you want. Please?" Angel's pleading look always pulled at my heartstrings. I couldn't refuse her request. I allowed her to take a few pictures and we noted a few details in her phone as well.

Angel wrapped her arms around me and kissed my cheek. "Talk to me about something good. Tell me about meeting Gavin." My wonderful friend knew me well, and she knew I wouldn't be able to dwell on the details without losing my shit. And there was nothing I hated to do more than cry.

"You know we met through Ashton."

"I know. Tell me about how you felt when you met him. Talk to me about your first date. I need some inspiration for my love quest."

I laughed at her choice of words. "Your love quest? You sound like you're Frodo on a mission or something." Angel smacked my arm. "I'll give you some advice. Don't hit men, and it will get you much further on the love quest."

She smacked me again. "Be serious."

"Okay, okay. I first spotted Gavin at a bar we hung out in a few years ago. He had a faux hawk and wore all black. My first thought was he could be the sexiest Emo I'd ever seen. Everything they say about tingles is true. He made me believe in love at first sight. Before I could walk up to him though, I saw Ashton walk over and hug him. Then I thought, how the hell do I compete with the Incredible Hulk?"

"Ashton is a beast of a man, isn't he?"

I nodded in agreement and continued my story. "Talking with him for five minutes though, I knew Ashton wasn't gay. It made me wonder why the hell Gracie thought he was for so long. Anyway, I finally got up the nerve to ask Gavin out after Gracie let it slip that he liked me. We clicked from the beginning, but our romance wasn't all roses and love poems. We have fought to be together from day one. Walking out in public holding hands is fine for a while, but eventually, you get the looks and the whispers, sometimes even disgusting words are thrown at you. Our first kiss was outside his house. It was one of those moments you read about in books where you knew this was the person you wanted to be with."

"I want that moment," Angel commented.

"When Gavin proposed to me, it was the happiest day of my life until I realized that we couldn't be married in our home state because it wasn't legal. When the Supreme Court made their decision on marriage equality, I thought, 'Finally we will be accepted in this country!' but I was wrong. I watched the verdict as it was announced, and I cheered and changed my profile pic on Facebook to a rainbow like so many other people. And then I saw the memes, and the stories of clerks denying the licenses in the name of their God. Reading comments from people who stated what a tragedy it was for the United States and we'd burn in hell for supporting gay marriage." As my voice choked on the words, I couldn't hold back the tears anymore. "I'm not ashamed to be gay, Angel, but I'm tired of having to defend who I am. Have you ever had to go into a job interview and explain your sex life? When I start a new job, I have a sit down with the boss to let them know I'm gay."

"Is it really necessary to tell them?" Angel asked.

"It's not a requirement, but it's easier than them figuring it out down the road. I've had bosses become very uncomfortable at the news and others embrace it without a care. And whether they will admit it or not, I've lost jobs because of it. There isn't much you can do in a 'right to fire' state without significant proof, and it's hard to prove bigotry."

Angel interrupted me by placing her hand over my mouth. "Stop talking, please. You were supposed to be talking about something happy and—"

It was my turn to cut her off. "I can't be the happy guy all the time!" I yelled louder than I meant to. My chest heaved with the emotion I had been desperately trying to hold back. Angel didn't jump back or become defensive. She grabbed my neck and pulled me into her arms in a strong embrace. The moment I felt the pressure of her arms around me, I lost it. I began to sob uncontrollably like the stupid pathetic side I try so desperately to hide on normal occasions. It's not the crying which made me pathetic but letting people take away my happiness based on their views of what I should be.

For the next few hours, I lay on the couch with my head in Angel's lap as she stroked my hair.

"I miss Gavin and Addy. I need to go home."

NINE

ANGEL

As the morning light invaded my bedroom, I rolled over with a groan and covered my face with a pillow. I had begun my descent back into dreamland when there was a knock on my door. "Go away," I mumbled. I wanted the holidays to be as uneventful this year as possible. Thanksgiving was over; I'd made it through without a hitch and had breezed through my year anniversary of sobriety, and now Christmas was beginning to invade. The hair and nail salon I worked in was in a mall, and this time of year was one of our busiest. Everyone wanted to look good for parties and seeing family. We'd begun working holiday hours and I hadn't gotten home until after midnight.

My request was ignored, and Tristan came into the room. "Good morning, sunshine." He plopped his annoying ass right next to me on the bed, and my whole body rolled toward him. "I need a favor, please."

More groaning came from me before I ripped the pillow away from my face and glared at him with an evil stare. "What?" I spat.

"Yikes. Do I need to get a Catholic priest and a crucifix in here? Are you going to spew pea soup?" As much help as Tristan gave me in the past year plus, I owed him any favors he asked. Not being a morning person, I couldn't help but snap when he stole away my few extra hours of sleep, but I dared not say no to his request.

I smacked his leg, and he chuckled. "I promised to help MJ with Katelyn's school Christmas party, and it's today. I apparently also agreed to decorate the bar for the holidays. Would you mind going to the bar to decorate for me?"

"Why don't I help MJ instead?"

"You don't really have the voice to play Santa convincingly. A hot Mrs. Claus for sure, but not the big man himself."

"Why isn't Derrick playing Santa?" I wasn't looking for excuses not to help Tristan, but going to the bar was not a good idea for me. Going to a grocery store tempted me to buy booze. Being in a place with it so readily available, I might as well reserve my spot for a second stint in rehab.

"He's meeting with the band manager for the group they're trying to get for the big New Year's Eve blast. It's a big deal and today was the only opening before the holidays." Nashville competed with

New York for attention on New Year's Eve celebrations by having their own version of the ball drop downtown. The celebration brought thousands to the area, making it a big deal for surrounding businesses to step it up. A Shot in the Dark was a relatively new kid on the block in comparison to some of the honky-tonk bars open for several decades.

"I know the bar isn't the ideal place, but you've been sober for over a year now and doing great. If it makes you feel better, I'll call some of the guys to come in and help and have one decorate the bar area." Every one of my friends made sacrifices for me to help with my sobriety. And in some way, every one of them was affected by the success or failure of the bar. Cameron, Ashton, Derrick, and Gavin owned it, which meant it affected Gracie and Mary Jane. Tristan was the head bartender, which meant it affected Macy and Lanie too. Anything I did for the bar was a favor to all of them.

I scoffed. "That's insulting to think I need a babysitter, T. I'll head over there in a bit, but send some of your hot bartenders over so I have spare hands." I may not need someone to watch me, but having people around would keep my focus off the alcohol surrounding me.

Tristan leaned forward and kissed my head. "Love you, A. MJ and I will be over as soon as we're done."

My drive to the bar was anxiety filled. Cold sweats, nausea, chest pain, dread, repeat. I had been sober for a year because I completely avoided being near readily available liquor. Now I was going to be in a place where there were bottles at my disposal. The night I'd gone to take care of Cameron was different. My friend was in need and nothing else mattered. But today, decorating the space, what would be my distraction from the seduction of the liquor bottles?

When I pulled into the parking lot, I took a deep breath and walked slowly to the door. As I fumbled for the keys, the door opened and Marcus stood there. My body betrayed me as a smile crept across my face when our eyes met. Struggling to make myself scowl, I said, "Hi. Are you my help or babysitter today?"

"Why would you need a babysitter?" Marcus asked, obviously oblivious to my alcohol issues or at least doing a great job of pretending.

"I'm sorry. Ninety percent of the time we've spent together has involved me snapping at you." I moved past him through the door and breezed across the room as far from the bar as possible.

"If you need to work on the percentage, I'm happy to spend more time with you." His grin was beyond adorable with the hint of a gleam in his eye.

I wasn't distracted by him for long enough. The liquor was all closed up in bottles, yet somehow I could smell the flavors. I could sense the sharp burn of the whiskey and taste the sweet foam of the beer on tap. Going to the bar had been a mistake.

The anxiety and stress of standing in the middle of an alcohol-infested space took a toll on my muscles. I inhaled sharply as pain coursed through my legs. Collapsing into a booth, I placed my head in my hands and tried to breathe through the pain.

Marcus slid into the booth across from me. "Is something wrong?" I didn't answer him. I felt his hand on my arm as he stroked my skin and asked, "Are you feeling sick?"

"My head hurts," I lied.

"I can do all of this by myself. I told Tristan, but I think he wanted a woman's touch. The truth is I grew up with six sisters and I'm probably the most feminine-thinking straight man in the world. I have better fashion sense than Cameron, though he'd never admit it."

I choked on a laugh that burst out of me. "You're right. He wouldn't admit it. I made a promise to Tristan, and I plan to keep it. I've put him through a lot in life, and this is the least I can do to help repay him. Where do we start?"

"I brought everything out of storage," Marcus said as he pointed over to a tall stack of boxes across the room. They were strategically placed right next to the bar. My stomach churned with apprehension of getting so close to the liquor.

"My headache is coming from neck pain and I'm not sure I can lift those boxes. Could you bring them over here for me?" A few lies seemed necessary in the situation. The little white lies to protect me, but not hurt anyone else.

Marcus asked no questions, so my lie must have been convincing enough. He lugged every box across the room until we were surrounded by decorations. We pulled the tree out first and placed it in the corner. Marcus began attaching the plugs to each section of the pre-lit tree while I fluffed out the branches to give it a fuller look. Grabbing a spindle from the box next to me, I unwrapped the string of red and gold pearls to drape across the limbs. Marcus reached up to help me, and when his hand covered mine, our eyes met. We stared at each other, my heart racing as I looked into his eyes. A moment straight from a romantic movie, something that never had happened to me in real life. I smiled and dropped my gaze when I realized how silly it was every time I saw the moment in a movie. As though one look, one touch from the opposite sex could mean they were your soul mate because of the thrill it ignited within you. One could just as easily chalk it up to lust.

Avoiding his gaze, I allowed him to finish the strings of pearls while I grabbed the next spool, which contained the silver-stringed tinsel. Strands of that stuff were the worst Christmas decoration ever invented, and I was thankful Cameron hated it as much as I did. As though he read my mind, Marcus commented, "There's none of that loose tinsel crap in the box is there?"

"No, why?"

"My sisters loved that shit, and it would end up everywhere in our house. I'd find it on my clothes, in the washer and dryer, even in the shower at times. When it came time to vacuum, those strings would cause the most unholy sounding screeching as they tangled within the machine. I swore I'd never even look at that stuff when I moved out."

"I hate it too. What was it like growing up with six sisters?"

"Being the youngest, they made me their guinea pig for several things." He chuckled and grabbed a handful of candy canes off the table next to him.

"Guinea pig? Oh, I need to hear examples of this." I reached out to grab a few canes myself to add to my side of the tree.

"My oldest sister would practice makeup tips on me. She's a manicurist now and I was her top client growing up. She learned how to make all the cute designs for nails by working on mine. I didn't mind though, it came off easily enough. The worst thing was when she did my makeup once, and I was so used to it, I forgot to wipe it off right away. A buddy of mine stopped by the house unannounced and spotted me all made up. He never let me live that one down." A sad look washed over his face briefly.

"Are you still close with your sisters?"

"They live in different parts of the country. We keep in touch via social media, but haven't gotten together as a family in a few years. Next year we're planning a big celebration for my oldest sister's fortieth birthday. I'll see them then. How about you? Siblings?"

"Brothers, two. We don't talk much anymore. Our family moved to Nashville when I was in grade school, and they were already both in high school. They were popular, I wasn't. We touched base with each other when I was living in Florida with MJ, but only briefly." Talking about my family wasn't something I enjoyed. After rehab, I called my parents to check in and let them know I was alive. Our relationship was better than before, but nowhere near perfect. My parents called occasionally, but mostly we kept in touch via the digital age. Texts, e-mail, social media likes, etcetera. My true family consisted of the friends I chose, Cameron, Gracie, Mary Jane, and everyone who came with them. We'd expanded our little family so much in the last few years, it was unbelievable. I was the last remaining single person in our family too.

Marcus lifted a box to place it on the table for us. I watched his arms flex into perfectly shaped muscles. A little bit of drool formed at the side of my mouth as I admired him. He turned toward me with a couple of ornaments in each palm. "Time for the final touches," he added.

There were very few regular ornaments to put up because most of them would be prizes to be given away throughout the year, an idea Cameron came up with to get extra business. A special box of clear numbered ornaments that would coincide with prizes was set to the side to go on last. Cameron loved Christmas so any chance he had to give presents, he took. He supplied gift cards and other prizes to the club. There were many ways to win. Some prizes would be awarded to a certain number at the bar, such as the one-hundredth customer of the night. Other prizes would be awarded for trivia nights to the person with the most correct answers.

I reached up to hang a crimson glass ball with gold sparkle designs when I felt a spasm in my arm. I shook it off and reached for another ornament made of silver beads shaped into a star. As I slid the ribbon over the branch, I felt a tug in my leg and it gave out from under me. I slumped forward hitting my face against the ladder before falling to the ground with a thud. Marcus had been on the other side of the room grabbing another box. He dropped it and came running. When the box hit the ground, the sound of shattering glass filled the room, and I cringed hoping it wasn't something important broken over me. Marcus grabbed a napkin container off the table and yanked several out as he knelt next to me. He reached forward to pat my nose with the napkin but pulled back suddenly. He handed the paper to me instead. "Your nose is bleeding. Do I need to call an ambulance?"

"I'm fine. Give me a few minutes to get over the embarrassment, and I'll get up." I couldn't stand until the spasms in my muscles stopped. I knew when they began it could take hours to overcome. I'm not a religious person, but I silently prayed this episode would pass quickly.

Marcus didn't argue. Instead, he lay next to me on the floor and stared up at the ceiling. "It's relaxing down here. I never noticed the lights look like stars up there. It's sort of romantic, don't you think?"

"Are you flirting with me?" I asked with a nasal tone in my voice.

My hands were pinching my nose through the napkin to staunch any bleeding. The romantic moment I'd imagined sharing with Marcus was much different.

"You're a beautiful woman with caramel skin, hair like silk, and an ass that won't quit. Why would I be flirting?" He winked, and his lip turned up in a half smile.

His description of me had me laughing and forgetting about the pain momentarily. I turned my head to look at him, and he smiled. "You have a great laugh too."

"Thanks. And thank you for the other night, with Cameron. It's not often our group gets help from outsiders." And again, I said something stupid and rude without considering my words first. Foot in mouth disease, another of my flaws.

"Ouch. What does it take to not be an outsider? I'm friends with most of you, and I shared a holiday meal." Marcus's face scrunched up in obvious hurt at my comment.

Awkwardly I fumbled an apology for my wording. "I didn't mean to make it sound like you weren't part of the group. We've all been together for so many years, I just...."

Marcus propped himself up on his elbow and began to move closer to me. I stopped talking and licked my lips as I awaited his kiss, but we were interrupted as the door opened and Tristan called out my name. Marcus jumped up first, and Tristan asked, "Why is Angel on the floor?"

"We had a little accident. She's fine though, she's getting her bearings."

Marcus went back to decorating while Tristan joined me on the floor. He lowered his voice to a whisper and asked, "Is this an MS moment?"

I nodded and fought back the tears. "I can't get up on my own. I don't want Marcus to see me struggle though. Can you send him on an errand or something?"

"Hey, Marcus, would you mind running to the back office and grabbing some ibuprofen for Angel, please?" As Marcus made his way across the floor, Tristan grabbed a bottle of water out of the cooler for me.

As soon as Marcus was out of the room, Tristan lifted me up into his arms, and I bit my lip to keep from screaming out. His fingers, though he was gentle, dug into my skin exacerbating the pain in my muscles. He placed me in a booth and kissed my forehead. "Is there something going on with you two?"

"No. I barely know him. He's cute though, and I like what I do know. I'd rather not scare him away with talk about my lifelong illness. I haven't been with a guy in over a year, and I want to date again. I want what the rest of you have. I'm tired of sleeping around and being the whore of the group."

"Stop it, Angel. You're not a whore. I would like to see you with a good guy though. Ask Marcus out, you two have a lot more in common than you know."

"I didn't mean Marcus necessarily. Anyway, how was the play?"

Marcus returned with the ibuprofen before Tristan could answer, and I downed four pills with the bottle of water he brought. The guys refused to let me continue decorating so I watched as they finished the job. Two hot guys stretching, exposing taut abs and happy trails disappearing into their jeans, it wasn't a bad sight to see. I focused more on Marcus's

body, but I wasn't oblivious to Tristan's sex appeal. We'd tangled in the sheets once, and though I don't remember it, I'm sure it was amazing. The thought of sleeping with him again was weird to me though. Not only because he's married to Lanie, but also the fact he's such a good friend of mine.

"Ta-da!" Tristan and Marcus shouted, pulling me from my thoughts. "How does it look?"

"Marcus, you weren't kidding, you have quite an eye for decorating."

Tristan scrunched up his face. "What am I chopped liver?"

"You did a spectacular job too, T." I squeezed his cheeks and gave him a quick kiss on the nose.

Marcus's lips formed a hard line of annoyance as he watched the display of affection I showed to Tristan. Jealousy was an adorable look on him; at least I hoped he was jealous. Although my romantic spiel to Tristan wasn't about Marcus, he wasn't ruled out as a possibility by any means.

TEN
CAMERON

Awaking to an empty bed was the worst way to start the day. The house was chilly since the temperature had slipped below freezing overnight. I slid my feet into my house shoes and shuffled into the hallway to check the heat settings. When I turned around to head to Addy's room, I spotted my family. Gavin had Addy in his arms and they were asleep together in the recliner. I never grew tired of seeing them like that. I plopped down in the chair across from them and watched their slumber.

A few moments later Gavin grumbled, "Even though we're married, it's still creepy when you watch me sleep. I could charge you with stalking."

I snorted. "I'm your husband and that gives me the legal right to stalk you."

"That's some deranged logic," Gavin replied.

"Were you not freezing? The temperature was so low on the thermometer I became a woman when I stepped out of bed. Cameron Jr crawled inside for warmth."

Gavin feigned disgust. "I can't be married to a woman, that's unnatural." He winked at me, and it gave my heart flutters like a lovesick teenager. "I didn't notice the cold, Addy's warmth kept me comfortable."

"How long have you been up?"

"She woke up crying a few hours ago. I think she had a bad dream."

"Do you want me to take her? Are you working today?" I stood up ready to take the snoring toddler from his arms.

"I want to spend the day with the two of you, if you're up for it." Gavin cocked an eyebrow as he made the offer, as though I'd be anything but excited.

"I'd love it! We haven't had a day together in a while."

Two hours later we were dressed and had Addy in a Disney T-shirt, pink with Minnie Mouse, a long-sleeved black undershirt, a pair of jeans with flowers embroidered on the pockets, and a headband covering her short curls. Disney outfits overflowed Addy's closet, courtesy of Mary Jane. During her pregnancy, while she was finishing her internship at Disney, she bought Addison outfits in every size from the parks. She also bought her enough coats to make it to her double-digit years. I zipped up her bright red parka and secured her hat; she looked like the little kid from *A Christmas Story*, Ralphie's brother. "Where are we going today?" I asked my adorable husband as he slid into the driver's seat after fastening Addy in securely.

Gavin set the GPS to the address for our favorite spot at Christmas, Cheekwood Gardens. He could get there with his eyes closed but liked the traffic and speed limit functions of the mapping tool. During the holidays, they had a display of trees decorated with different themes, and at night, the outside was brightly lit in a colorful display. "I went by the club the other day and saw the decorations, it looks great. Did you and Derrick do that?"

"Nope. Angel and Marcus decorated for us. I think Tristan helped a little too."

"Angel?" Gavin asked with surprise. I could see the wheels turning as he ran thoughts through his mind. "You set her up?"

I smirked. No one knew me better than Gavin. Gracie came close, but he'd surpassed her since she'd been with Ashton. "They're both single, former players, who desperately need to get laid. Angel was covering for Tristan and had asked for help. All I did was call the other bartenders to see who was available. It's not my fault the first one I called was Marcus, and he was free."

Gavin laughed and replied with deep sarcasm, "You're such a romantic."

"I am a romantic, you know that first hand. When it comes to Angel though, she doesn't want romance. She's always been a wham-bam-thank-you-ma'am kind of girl."

Gavin's tone became serious with his reply. "Maybe she wants it now. Talk to her before you set her up to fall for a guy who wants her for sex and nothing else. She's been through so much in the last year or so."

"I did talk to her. She says she wants the real thing for a change, and I hope she means it. Marcus is a nice guy. He's the one who asked me about dating her. I think he's ready to settle down." Marcus had confided in me recently about how he didn't want to sleep around anymore. At some point in life, I believed everyone got tired of the hassle of dating new people. I never reached the point of it being a hassle, but I was lucky to find my prince early in life. The night after they decorated the club, Marcus confided in me about how attracted he was to Angel and wanted to know what I thought about them dating. In that moment, I knew I'd made the right decision pushing them to spend time together.

"Still, you should talk to Angel. She has a lot going on right now, and you don't want to stress her out or affect her sobriety." I knew he was right. Angel had risen far above her problems, but she was still close to the edge with the danger of falling off at any time.

I sighed in defeat. "Fine. I'll talk to her. Can we enjoy our family day now?"

Gavin grabbed my hand and kissed it. "You're a good friend. I should've said that before I criticized your choice. I love you."

"I know," I replied with a teasing roll of my eyes.

Meddling in my friends' lives was something I had a knack for, I admit. During one of my first dates with Gavin, I arranged for Gracie to spend time with Ashton.

Gavin had been with Ashton most of the day. I hadn't realized the importance of their time together until Gavin picked me up in the evening to hang out. We were meeting our friend Xander for a double date with his guy of the moment. Gavin and Ashton had spent the day shopping and happened upon the bookshop with the café where Gracie was a barista. In the car, Gavin had been telling me about their day, the anniversary of his sister Addison's death.

Ashton was always miserable on the date, and Gavin made a promise to his sister's memory that he would help him get past the grief in appreciation for all Ashton's family had done for him. "I don't know what it is about Gracie, but Ashton lights up around her," Gavin told me. He reached out and took my hand in his. "She seems to have the same effect on him as you have on me." No one had made me blush as hard as Gavin.

"I want everyone to feel the way you make me feel." Taking out my phone, I sent a quick text to Ashton.

Me: Do you think you could go by and check on Gracie tonight? She gets off around ten, and I worry about her walking alone.

Ashton: You don't think she would be weirded out?

Me: Not when she sees it's you. Don't tell her I sent you back

though. She hates when I worry.

A few hours later, and about three piña coladas to the wind, I received a text from Gracie.

Gracie: Ash surprised me at work tonight. He's following me on his bike and we're going to dinner. Didn't want you to worry if you tried me at home.

Cameron: Have fun, slut puppy.

I told Gavin all about my plan, and he offered a high five for my matchmaking skills. We both had our friends' happiness in mind, and it just happened the two of them could make each other happy. They only needed a little push.

As we were getting ready to leave the bar, Gavin grabbed me by the wrist and pulled me against him. His lips met mine in a tender kiss at first that quickly became more heated. Catcalls and whistles from the street brought us out of the spell for a moment. "I have an idea," Gavin smirked with a wink. He sent a text, and a few minutes later, he pumped his fist in the air. "Two love-birds, one stone."

"What did you do?"

"Texted Ash to pick our drunk asses up." I'd never seen Ashton drive anything, but a motorcycle and my intoxicated mind couldn't comprehend how we'd all fit on it with him. "You look like you're thinking too hard. You said he's with Gracie, right?" I nodded. "Gracie has a car. From what you've told me about her, she'll offer to come pick us up instead. And Ashton would never let her drive downtown at night

alone. He's too much of a gentleman."

"You're a meddler like me. I think I love you." And the make-out session resumed. We lost all track of time, and my lips were going numb from the contact. Neither of us would have been so intimate in public if we'd been sober. Gracie's voice yelled out, "Get it, girl." She used my own line on me, so I saluted her with my favorite finger, the middle one.

"Cameron, where did you go, love?" Gavin waved his hand in front of my face.

"Sorry, I was thinking about how we set up Ashton and Gracie. She had no idea how vital we were in bringing them together. It's time we work our magic on Marcus and Angel." If they ended up even half as happy as Ashton and Gracie were, they'd be grateful for our interfering. I knew Marcus well enough to know he wouldn't hurt Angel the way other men had in the past.

A couple of days after our outing, I went back to work ready to set my plan in motion. As I tried to focus on work and put the matchmaking aside for later, the door opened.

"Can we talk?" Marcus walked into my office and shut the door. I was supposed to have been working on the designs for an extension to the party room, but I couldn't concentrate. I'd been playing around on Facebook for a half hour ignoring reality.

The club didn't open for another hour, so I moved over to the couch to sit with him. "What's up?" He sat twiddling his thumbs nervously, not speaking for a few minutes. Marcus had never been one to be lacking in things to say. "Is this about Angel?"

"Kind of. Last time I tried to talk to you, we were interrupted. I could use some friendly advice." While talking, he scrolled through his phone looking for something in particular it seemed. Turning it toward me, he said, "This is my friend Calvin."

"He's the one who's been sick? You never told me what his diagnosis was."

"He's HIV positive." Stunned wasn't an understatement on how I took the news. As a homosexual male, let me rephrase, as a *responsible* homosexual male, I regularly had myself tested up until Gavin and I had been married for over a year. We waited to make sure we were both out of any risk range before taking a chance with one another. We may not have to worry about babies like heterosexual couples, but we had much worse things to fear. As a gay man, HIV was something on my mind often. The disease passed so rampantly through the gay community because too many disliked using condoms and felt it wasn't a big deal to forego them since pregnancy wasn't a concern. In my case, I'd never ridden bareback until marrying Gavin.

"Wow. So how does his diagnosis affect you? Did you two…?"

"No!" the word came out with great defense. "No offense, I just mean I've never been with a guy before."

"I was going to ask if you two had slept with the same girl." His jump to a conclusion didn't offend me. Though HIV was most rampant in the gay community, heterosexuals were not risk free. The statistics were crazy, more than sixty percent of cases are male to male contact while only a little more than twenty percent are heterosexual. The other percentages fall into intravenous drug users. As if being a gay man wasn't hard enough with the judgment, having to hide who we were for fear of rejection, the promise of damnation, all of this daily, plus worrying about the disease.

"If this is too personal, tell me to shut up. Have you ever been tested?" The first time I'd been asked about HIV testing was after Gracie's rape. We'd never broached the subject before her attack. After, in private, she asked me to go with her to be tested when three months had passed from her initial test.

"Of course. It would be irresponsible for me to not have. Before Gavin, I always wore condoms, but they aren't infallible. So I was tested twice a year. Gavin and I continued the tradition until our one-year anniversary." We celebrated our one-year anniversary by throwing out condoms and swearing we'd never have to be tested again. We were literally trusting each other with our lives.

"Would you...." His words trailed off and his glance fell to the floor. Vulnerability wasn't something Marcus wore often.

"Go with you?" I finished what I assumed was the question he struggled to ask. Marcus nodded. "Absolutely. We can go first thing in the morning if you want. The health center takes walk-ins and," I glanced at my watch, "they closed an hour ago so we can't go tonight."

"Tomorrow's perfect. Before I ask Angel out, I want to be sure I'm not putting her in danger."

Telling my friend's business was never something I did. In this case, it seemed the right thing to do. So for the next few minutes, I filled Marcus in on Angel's diagnosis of multiple sclerosis. The alcoholism was something she'd have to tell him. However, the fact he struggled with the possibility of a disease like AIDS, I needed him to see the—mostly—full picture of what Angel dealt with daily. Stress was a trigger for pain, and worrying about what could have been was the last thing she needed.

The Lentz Public Health Center in Nashville offered testing at a minimum charge based on income. Marcus appeared nervous to say why he was there, as though he expected judgment, criticism, or possibly fear. The woman behind the desk handed him paperwork without flinching, seemingly putting the nervous man at ease for the moment. Taking a seat in the far corner of the room, he began thumbing through his paperwork.

"Wow. Some of my closest friends don't know these intimate details about my sex life." Paperwork for testing was essentially an invasion of privacy. Those little things you like to try in the bedroom with partners, but you don't tell your friends about because they might judge you, well you had to write them down. And if you tested positive, I'd seen it happen to acquaintances, you made a list of all your lovers. For Marcus, I imagine this would be more paper than the registration itself.

"I know it's a lot to take in, but don't worry, they don't publish it in the paper or anything. It's still between you and your doctor. I promise not to peek at your freakdom." His look of horror dissipated when I gave him a wink.

Setting the pen down, he scrubbed his hands over his face. "What do I do if it comes back positive? Does this affect my job?"

"First, your job is safe. I double-checked the laws after you told me. As for your personal life, you contact everyone possible and take your meds and most importantly, you keep living. As scary as it is, Marcus, they have come so far in the treatment of HIV and AIDS. It's not like in the eighties when people died right and left from it. The meds can help you live a long happy life."

"A long lonely life." Defeated he leaned his head back against the wall.

"It's not a vow of abstinence. It means you use condoms, and you never go without them because you forgot or it feels better. It's not a death sentence unless you make it one." If Marcus tested positive, we'd have to let the other guys know for health reasons at the bar, just in case there was an accident. I knew the price of the medicine would be hard for him to afford. We paid well, but those meds ran quite high. Worst-case scenario, I'd take up the cost of the meds for him. And a positive wouldn't necessarily mean he couldn't be with Angel. I would insist he tell her up front. She deserved the chance to make the choice herself of whether to pursue a relationship further.

"All I can think about is Angel. It's not love; we barely know each other. But, it's something. Every time I lay eyes on her, something happens. My heart beats faster, my mood lifts. She's like a natural high for me. And I don't want some stupid one-night stand to ruin my chance at getting to know her better." Going through life, we all eventually meet someone who makes us happy, whether it's a friend or a significant other. Hearing someone speak about Angel as their person of happiness, brightened my day. As her friend, I'd watched her go through more heartache than anyone deserved, all in a short time. Some of it she brought on herself of course, but it didn't mean she deserved any of it.

Reaching down deep inside, I pulled out the character I put on when my friends need it most. "Child, please. Stop freaking out about this mess and go on in there and get your blood drawn. You act like your dick has shriveled up and fallen off and life is over. Fill out this damn paperwork, march in there, and get this shit done." I hoped he would understand I was using tough love to prepare him. After a moment he stood up, walked the paper over to the woman, and came back to sit next to me until they called his name a minute later.

Within only a few minutes, he was back out of the room with a handful of pamphlets to read over and a look of relief on his face. "Well, that's done. Now I just wait up to three days for the results. How do I get through the next few days without having a meltdown?"

Placing my arm across his shoulder, I put on my serious voice again. "Booze. And lots of it." He eyed me curiously, and I chuckled. "I'm kidding, man. You come to me when you're worried, and I'll talk you down. It's what friends do."

ELEVEN

ANGEL

Since decorating at the club two weeks ago, I hadn't seen or heard from Marcus. I don't know why I expected to; we hadn't exchanged numbers. If he wanted me, he could've asked Tristan or Cameron for my number, and the same could be said about me. I thought about showing up at the club to see him, but it was a terrible idea for me to be around so much alcohol.

He was on my mind so much lately, I began to feel obsessed. I knew so little about him, but I wanted him close to me. It may have been the lack of sex in my life or perhaps the fact I was constantly surrounded by happily married couples. I kept imagining what our kiss would have been like if Tristan hadn't interrupted. Every time I closed my eyes, I could smell his cologne and feel the heat of his body next to mine. As I lay in bed, I imagined taking things to the next step. Scooting down the bed, I pulled the covers close to my head as my hand slipped beneath them. Before I could remove my panties, my fantasy was interrupted.

"Angel!" Macy called out from down the hall. I struggled to get out of bed and make it to the door. I cracked the door open and heard, "Come downstairs, we need your opinion."

Macy, Tristan's highly intelligent younger sister, was home for Christmas break from college life. Lying in bed had been so comfortable I hadn't realized how much pain I was about to experience. I held onto the banister tightly as I moved slowly downstairs. My muscles were not my friends today, and every step shot pain up through my limbs. Macy ran to the bottom step and reached for me. She escorted me to the couch and helped me sit down.

"What do you need my opinion on?" I glanced around the room and saw Lanie sitting at the desk with the laptop open.

"I'm sorry, Angel. We should've come upstairs to you," Lanie said as she witnessed my struggle.

"It's fine. I never know when the pain will hit me, you can't possibly know that either."

"We're shopping for houses, and we have it narrowed down to two choices." Macy leaned over Lanie's shoulder and began to list the qualities of both houses. A sudden feeling of nausea rushed over me. Our lease ran out on this house in a few months, and I had to find a place to live. I could afford to live on my own, but the scary part was I wouldn't have the support system I'd had with my roommates.

I pulled myself out of my thoughts and glanced up to see Macy staring at me. "Well, which one do you think?"

Lanie's eyes were fixed on mine and she cleared her throat before shutting her laptop. "Let's look at this later when Tristan is home. Macy, can you give us a moment?"

Macy left the room, and Lanie asked me to sit with her. "You're scared of us moving, aren't you?"

"No. You deserve to have a house of your own. You don't need me hanging around with you two newlyweds. I'll be fine." Tristan and Lanie almost lost each other over my living situation before. I wouldn't cause them any more trouble. The first time they were engaged, Lanie asked Tristan to move in with her, and he told her he couldn't because of me. Assuming his feelings were stronger for me than he knew, Lanie broke off the engagement and they spent five months apart. After their reunion, Lanie and Tristan came to an agreement. She sold her house, moved in with him, and they would use the money on a down payment for a house after they were married. There was no way I'd interfere with them now.

Lanie grabbed my hands and held them tightly. "We're going to always be your family, Angel. I know you've had a rough time with the alcoholism and the MS. We're not abandoning you. In fact, Tristan has been looking for homes with enough rooms to include you. We wanted to talk to you together about it. We also found a house with a detached garage with a room over it. You'd have your privacy and still have our support. We'll even arrange a rental agreement for you."

"What about Macy? She should get the special room. She's in college and deserves privacy."

"She's in college living in a dorm room. She doesn't need a full-time place from us. We'll make sure to get a house big enough for her to have a bedroom of her own for the times she's home. Please think about it. We love you, Angel." When Tristan and Lanie first reconciled, things were awkward between us. She moved in and we shuffled around each other in the mornings, staying out of one another's way. One day things exploded.

Lanie opened the door of the bathroom and bumped straight into me wearing only a towel. I'd forgotten to lock the bathroom door and was so surprised, I jumped and lost my grip on the towel. Tristan walked into the hallway as my towel fell and I quickly grabbed it to cover myself. Her head whipped around to catch Tristan's mouth agape. "This isn't going to work!" she exclaimed, exasperated. She'd been tiptoeing around me since the moment she moved in with us. I offered to leave and find my own place, but she was too polite to say she didn't want me there. I knew the tension had been building and I tried to stay out of her way. I liked Lanie, but I understand why she was hesitant to trust me. She'd seen me at my worst, and I had inadvertently caused trouble in her relationship with Tristan.

Heartbroken, Tristan reached forward and grabbed Lanie's shoulders. "Please don't leave me again. We'll make this work." Shaking her head as the tears fell, she refused to listen to him and stormed away slamming the door behind her. Tristan's hands pulled at his hair as he stared at the door, grief clouding his features.

I tried to reach for him, but my hand never made contact as he walked forward. Just before he closed the door, I saw Lanie packing her bags. Running to my bedroom, I quickly put on clothes knowing I had to make things right. Loud voices filled the hallway, making me thankful Macy was away at school and missed their fight. Tapping the door with my knuckles, I called out, "Can I come in please?" Both voices yelled out a 'No,' but I ignored them.

"Please, let me speak to Lanie alone?" I begged Tristan. Lanie sighed and nodded toward him. He trudged out of the room with his shoulders slumped.

"You're wasting your breath. Nothing you can say will change anything, Angel. This will never work." Her acrid tone left me feeling hopeless at changing her mind.

"You weren't here, Lanie. You didn't see what Tristan went through without you. He was miserable. Even though he had every right to, he never took his misery out on me. You won't find a better man in the world than Tristan. My only hope is I'll be as lucky to find someone so wonderful." Since she'd moved in, Lanie had made every effort to be friends with me, but with everything going on in my life, I hadn't given

as much in return to make it easier for her.

Lanie dropped the clothes into the suitcase, placed her hands on the bed, and sighed. "What is the point of telling me this?"

"I'll move out. Give me two weeks to find a place, and I'm gone."

"You'd do that? For Tristan?"

"I'd do that for both of you. You make him happy. I owe him my life, and you are what he wants most. We never have to be friends. But don't leave him."

Lanie stepped toward me. "I have a better idea. I'll give this a month, but not for you to find a place. We're going to spend time together and become friends. You can't be the only one offering up sacrifices here." She held out her hand, and I shook it. For the next month, we scheduled girl dates twice a week, and by the end of it, we'd worked out our issues and become friends.

"I almost caused you two to break up. Why would you want me around?"

Lanie chuckled and shook her head. "That was a long time ago, and it wasn't your fault." She changed the subject abruptly. "I heard you spent some time with Marcus the other day."

"What? I mean, yeah sure. Why?"

"No reason. He's cute though, right?" Lanie said, nudging me with her elbow. I rolled my eyes at how adolescent this moment felt. She was wiggling her eyebrows and winking at me over a boy like she wanted to ask me if I wanted to go steady with him.

"He's easy on the eyes." As many times as we'd been in the same place, it seemed someone was working overtime to put us together. "Are you and Tristan trying to set me up?"

"Do you like him?" Lanie asked as though waiting for me to giggle and blush, denying my schoolgirl crush. Marcus was quite possibly the most beautiful specimen of man I'd laid eyes on in a long time. He had a certain charm, and I had imagined what his hands and other parts of his body would feel like on my skin. In a way, I craved him, which could present a problem. If I became too attached to him and it didn't work out, it could affect my recovery. It'd been over a year since I had a drink and a man; what happened when I caved and gave myself over to one?

"I need to get dressed and get to work." Noticing her look of disappointment, I sighed and added, "I appreciate you looking out for me."

After work, I had offered to watch Craig for Mary Jane and Derrick so they could enjoy a night out. Their daughter Katelyn had a sleepover with her Girl Scout troop, and being the single friend who had no interest in clubbing anymore, I volunteered to babysit often.

Mary Jane opened the door and yanked me inside without a word. "What the…" I spat before I got a good glimpse at her. "Oh shit.

What the hell happened to you?" Her hair was curly on one side and a frizz ball on the other. Her mascara left black streaks down her face. I began to panic. "Have you been attacked?"

"Only by a rogue curling iron and a curling brush! I had to cut the brush from my hair after it left me with this!" She cried pointing at the frizz ball side of her head. "Derrick will be home any minute, and this is our first night out together in months. I can't go out looking like this!" Her voice became higher pitched with each word and the tears wouldn't stop.

"Calm down, MJ. Go wash your face and rinse your hair. I've got a home remedy I'll put together to get out the frizz, and I'll even up the cut. We'll have you fixed up in no time."

Derrick walked in about five minutes later and I told him I needed to help Mary Jane with her hair, without telling him the disaster it had been. He grabbed Craig up from the playpen and began a playful conversation with his son.

Mary Jane sat on the toilet (lid closed) with a towel wrapped around her head. She wore nothing but a slip and pantyhose while her dress hung from the shower rod. "Derrick is keeping Craig busy. Do you have leave-in conditioner?"

Mary Jane pointed to the bottom cabinet of the sink. "We keep some in there for Katelyn's hair." Normally I could whip up something from the kitchen with a few things from the pantry, but the conditioner was a lot easier. I spritzed her hair generously and began to work through the tangles. Lucky for me, Mary Jane wasn't tender headed because I yanked at her hair roughly.

"Where are you two going tonight?"

"We're going to Derrick's favorite steakhouse for dinner and then to a movie. Oh, and Marcus may stop by to drop off some paperwork for the club."

My hand left her head and went to my hip as I let out an exaggerated sigh. "Seriously, you too?"

"Me too, what?" Mary Jane asked with sincere confusion.

"Are you trying to set me up with Marcus like Cameron, Tristan, and Lanie?" I'd never needed help landing a man before, nor had my friends concerned themselves so much with my love life. With everyone being coupled up and having babies, I supposed I stuck out like a white shirt under a black light.

"Oh," she said a bit confused and then with clarity, she exclaimed, "Oh! No, but that's a great idea. We love Marcus. He's been helping fill in for Tristan lately, as assistant manager." And now I'd given her an idea to pursue with the rest of my friends. I could see the wheels turning as her eyes sparkled.

The frizz ball was gone. I trimmed the edges to correct the spot she had to cut. I gathered her hair and twirled it into a French twist holding it with a gold barrette. Leaving around three inches of hair spilling out the top, I used the curling iron to give it a good bounce. Once I finished her 'do, I gave her makeup a few last-minute touchups and turned her toward the mirror.

"Angel, you're a goddess. I look beautiful." She turned her head from side to side admiring her reflection.

"You make it easy on a girl. You're always beautiful," I said as I kissed her cheek. "Now go have a wonderful evening with your sexy husband. Feel free to stay out as late as you want. I brought everything I need to keep me entertained after Craig goes to bed." A Kindle, Netflix subscription, and a smartphone could keep anyone sufficiently entertained for days, even months.

When Derrick saw Mary Jane, his mouth fell open and his eyes lit up. It gave me butterflies to see the love he felt for her. I craved my own happily ever after almost as much as alcohol lately. Derrick strolled to Mary Jane, placed his hands on her cheeks, and kissed her with passion, making me blush at witnessing the intimate moment.

I cleared my throat and grumbled teasingly, "Get a room."

Derrick laughed. "Thank you, Angel, for giving us this evening out."

"Take full advantage of it. I brought my Kindle loaded with books, and I plan on raiding your movie cabinet as well."

The moment they left, Craig began to cry. I lifted him from the playpen and sang to him until he calmed down. We curled up on the couch together, and I searched through Netflix until I found a movie to watch.

Craig drifted to sleep within minutes of the movie starting, but I held him until it was over. I enjoyed the comforting feel of him in my arms. Babies were not in my foreseeable future. I didn't ever see myself as mom material. I loved other people's children though. When I was younger, I never thought I'd settle down, so children were an impossible idea. Then, after the MS diagnosis and the alcoholism, it seemed a lot for anyone to handle.

I could have sat there with him all night if my bladder wasn't about to burst. I placed him in his crib and ran to the restroom.

Before I finished, the doorbell rang, and I begged out loud for it not to wake Craig. Quickly I ran my hands under scalding hot water, burning at least the first layer of skin off. Cursing under my breath, I ran to the door and flung it open. Marcus stood there poised to ring the doorbell again. He took one look at the scowl on my face and pulled his hand back. "Yikes, is this a bad time?"

"Shhh," I hissed before yanking him through the door. "The baby is sleeping." The little man never flinched, saving Marcus from a kick in the nuts.

"Sorry," he whispered. He held his hands out with a folder full of paperwork. "Derrick needed this for some reason tonight."

I rolled my eyes and said, "They're trying to set us up. All these little moments we've been running into each other have all been part of a grand scheme. I apologize for my friends."

Marcus smirked. "Well, they're my friends too. Is it a bad thing they want to set us up? I mean, we're two very good-looking individuals, and I can swear to you I've never committed a crime or been in a mental institution. I have moles in some weird places, but who doesn't."

I guffawed at his honesty. "I have a mole in the exact middle of my left butt cheek," I replied.

"I don't believe you. I need you to prove it," Marcus stated matter-of-factly.

Again, I laughed at him. It had been a long time since I felt so comfortable laughing. It was a sound I barely recognized anymore. "You'll have to buy me dinner first."

He pulled a cell phone from his pocket and asked, "Do you like Chinese?"

"Love it."

The next words out of his mouth were to the person on the phone as he ordered a slew of Chinese items and rattled off his credit card number for payment. When he hung up, he pushed my jaw back up to close my mouth. "Hope you're hungry."

TWELVE

ANGEL

arcus had ordered all my favorite things somehow. "Did you set this up with MJ or Derrick?"

"No. This was a spur of the moment decision. Why?"

"How did you know my favorite foods?" I asked.

"I didn't. I ordered all my favorites." His answer made me swoon harder over this muscular god in front of me. I didn't know what to say to him. "Um, I'll get us some drinks."

"Soda or water for me please, I have to drive home." Again, he assumed I wanted alcohol. I wasn't sure what kind of vibes I gave off to this man.

"Sweet tea? MJ made some for me, her tea is the best." No point in yelling at the poor man again. He'd explained to me before it was based on his career as a bartender, and I had to stop being paranoid.

"Perfect," he said, smiling at me.

Bracing myself against the counter, I took a deep breath and tried to get my nerves under check. I hadn't been this nervous with a guy, well, ever. I was like a girl hitting puberty discovering boys made her tingle down below. Once I gathered my courage to go face him again, I grabbed the freshly poured teas and met him in the living room. I'd been in there longer than I realized because he was paying the Chinese deliveryman.

I gazed around the room noticing he'd lit a few candles and dimmed the lighting in a smooth move. I'd never been romanced before; I could get used to it. He turned and smiled, his gleaming white teeth adding even more glow to the room.

"I like what you did in here."

Marcus blushed a little when he asked, "I hope I didn't go overboard?" I shook my head. Overboard was probably an accurate word for most people who saw this, but I wanted all the bells and whistles of romance.

We sat down to eat, and I picked up the chicken lo mein first attempting to eat it with chopsticks. When I dropped the food down in my shirt, straight into my bra, Marcus leaned forward and said, "Let me clean that up for you." I swatted his hand away playfully when he reached out as though he were going to touch my breast.

I leaned forward to grab a napkin from the table, used it to clean up the noodles, and reached to place it in the empty bag. Marcus leaned forward, our faces inches apart and declared, "I want to kiss you." He waited patiently for my response. My heart raced as I closed the distance between us. The moment our lips met, a surge of electricity rushed through my body. His lips tasted sweet from the teriyaki sauce. When I opened my mouth slightly, he took it as an invitation and slid his tongue between my lips. I moaned and shifted my body to move closer to him. His hand dipped between my legs, but it was to take the box of food and move it. Once all the obstacles were out of the way, he moved over me pushing me back on the couch. My mind was screaming for me to slow down, but my body wasn't listening. A gorgeous man was kissing me, and I hadn't felt wanted in that way in so long that I couldn't stop myself. For the past year, I thought I could handle anything, but lust was a force to be reckoned with.

One hand trailed down the side of my body until it reached the hem of my shirt. Soft hands ventured inside my shirt, my stomach trembled with the light touches. His excitement pressed against my core, and I gasped with the pull of desire in my stomach. The thoughts of needing to stop weren't traveling from my brain to my mouth or body because I lifted my hips to grind against his erection, eliciting a groan from his lips. *Damn, it had been too long since I had been with a man.* My body was on fire. My hands tugged his shirt from his pants and slid inside to graze his muscular chest. Our hips met thrust for thrust as we dry humped each other through our clothes. I was close to getting off without even being naked. Just when his hand pushed my bra away and cupped my breast, the baby cried out. *Fuck.* I'd let myself get carried away, like old times.

I pushed Marcus away, jumped up, and ran to check on Craig without a word to him. Adjusting my bra as I went, I sighed in annoyance. I needed to come back to reality, I had to push the old Angel back out. No "wham bam thank you, ma'am" tonight. It was time for me to have more. I wanted to be loved.

"Hey, baby boy, what's the matter?" I cooed as I lifted him out of the crib. My nose scrunched up when I got a whiff of what was wrong with him. Once he was cleaned up, I rocked him for a few minutes and he fell to sleep again.

Back in the living room, Marcus sat on the couch patiently waiting for my return. I had hoped he'd left while I was changing the baby. As I sat down, he stood up. "I need to go, but I wanted to say goodbye first. Look, what happened was a mistake. I—"

I interrupted him. "What happened was, you were dropping paperwork off, and I will make sure Derrick gets it." I walked over and held the door open waiting for him to leave. He seemed as regretful about what we did as I was, but I didn't want to hear his excuses. I refused to resort back to my old ways.

Marcus stood in the doorway and turned back toward me. "All I was trying to say is, it was a mistake for us to move so fast. I'm grateful

Craig interrupted us when he did. But, I know you want me as much as I want you. The way you kissed me, how your body warmed to my touch, it was undeniable. When you're ready to continue getting to know each other, call me. You know how to get my number."

I closed the door behind him and a shiver coursed through my body. He was right; I wanted him more than I was willing to admit out loud.

Mary Jane and Derrick came home late and asked me to spend the night. They were worried I'd be too tired to drive home. The next morning, I woke up in a sweat on the couch after a vivid dream about Marcus. The embarrassment came when my eyes met with Derrick's a moment after waking. He smirked and blushed when he asked, "Good dream?"

Sitting up in a rush, I pushed my hair off my face. "What? Why do you ask?"

"You were twisting roughly and moaning fairly loudly. Does this have anything to do with Marcus stopping by yesterday? Did you hit it off?" We'd almost had sex on the very spot I was currently sitting. Hitting it off was an understatement.

A text saved me from the awkward conversation. "I have to go. I'm covering a coworker's shift today."

Grabbing my things in a hurry, I ran out the door with Derrick calling out, "We'll continue this later!" I waved goodbye without a word. *Oh no, we won't!*

My friends meant well, and I appreciated their concern, but I needed to live my life a certain way. I wanted what seemed impossible. I wanted a date with a man ending in a simple goodnight kiss that was soft and sweet. Then I wanted a second date where we were awkward and nervous after sharing a kiss. All I ever got was the guy who wanted to jump my bones before we even had a real date. I didn't mind before, but I was ready for something profound, the kind of love story people envy. I loved sex, but I deserved love. I desired an answer to the question of whether loving someone made the sex better. I'd never been in love, and I wanted, no I needed that to change.

THIRTEEN

CAMERON

"**M**ove out of the way! Ugh, Nashville drivers are the worst." I swerved in and out of traffic trying to get behind someone doing the speed limit instead of going twenty miles below.

"Calm your tits, Cameron. We're not going to be late," Angel said from the passenger seat without glancing up from her phone.

"Speed up, Fuckrod!" I shouted at the car in front of me.

Angel snorted with laughter and said, "I think that would be a dick. Leave it to you to come up with a word for dick that sounds even naughtier."

"Hmm, you're right. I don't even know where the word Fuckrod came from. It popped into my head. I sometimes have spontaneous

Tourette's."

Angel snorted again. "Spontaneous Tourette's is not a thing. Do you need to pull over and let me drive?"

"I got this, I got this," I said with as much assurance as possible. We were on our way to the airport to pick up Gavin. He'd been on a business trip for almost a month, he left the day after Christmas, and I couldn't wait to wrap my arms around his beautiful self. I needed to take my mind off the drive, so it would go by faster. "So, Marcus asked about you."

"Hmm," Angel responded pretending to be nonchalant.

"He wanted your number. He said you were supposed to ask Derrick for his, but since you weren't calling, he wanted to call you." Based on how desperate he was for her number I could only assume they'd connected on their last meeting. Derrick, Tristan, and I were tag teaming as matchmakers on this one. With the rest of us living our happily ever after, we wanted Angel to find hers. So what if we gave her a little push toward Marcus? They were practically the same person; it seemed a no-brainer.

"And you told him no, this isn't eighth grade, and he can ask me for my phone number or take rejection like a man. Right?" A spitfire attitude was one of Angel's sexiest qualities.

I scoffed. "Sure, I told him exactly that. Please, I'm not a douchebag. I programmed your number into his phone."

Angel spun around in her seat, and I could feel the fierce look.

"You all have to stop trying to set me up! I'm a grown woman—"

I cut her off. "A grown woman who hasn't had sex in over a year! Little Miss is probably all dried up down there."

"You are so gross sometimes, Cam," she said with a laugh. At least I knew she wasn't too angry with me. I had my reasons for wanting her and Marcus together. Angel quit guys when she went into rehab and Marcus quit women about five months ago. They both had been through something that made them feel the need to cut themselves off from everyone. Knowing what Marcus was struggling with, I knew he and Angel could help each other.

Marcus had slept with women on a regular basis, and I'd barely seen him flirt with anyone lately. Before he opened up to me about Calvin, I asked him about the lack of women in his presence. He gave me the same crap answer Angel gives everyone, "I'm trying to get my life in order and don't need the distraction of a relationship." The reason I knew it was crap was neither of them ever had relationships. If they charged for all the sex they'd had in life, they'd both be rich.

His first HIV test had come back negative, but they always advise a second test three months later to be sure. The load of stress didn't seem to lighten with the first set of results. Asking for Angel's number was a good sign he was getting back in the dating scene though.

I had to put on my serious voice, a voice I hated to use. "Angel, Marcus is a good guy, scratch that, he's a great guy. You have so much in common it's insane. If you had a penis or he had a vagina, I'd think you were the same person."

"I am a recovering alcoholic with multiple sclerosis. That's a lot of baggage to bring into a relationship with a great guy. I'm rejecting him for myself as much as I am for him." No matter what excuses she gave, I knew deep down Angel was terrified of being hurt again.

"Shouldn't he be given the chance to reject you if he thinks he can't handle it? Maybe if you tell him the truth, you'd be surprised at his reaction."

Angel stared out the window without answering.

"I heard you shared a pretty hot kiss."

She reached up and touched her lips as a small smile appeared there.

"I saw that shit eating grin. You thought it was hot too!"

Angel exhaled with frustration. "I'll admit his kisses made me…"

"Made your nether regions gush like Niagara Falls?" I always tried to be as crass as possible to lighten the mood.

"Eww, Cameron!" she exclaimed, smacking my arm. "He's a good kisser. Period. We're not discussing anything else, especially my nether regions."

"You need a hefty dose of bow-chick-a-bow-wow, chica. I'm just looking out for you and Little Miss's best interest."

"Stop referring to my vagina as Little Miss!"

"What do you call her?" I asked.

"A vagina."

"That's disgusting," I said, cringing dramatically. "It's too textbook sounding. Would you want me going around calling Cameron Jr. a penis?"

"Oh the horror of calling it by its true name," Angel replied sarcastically.

"Its true name is Cameron Jr. Any male genitalia can be a penis. It takes a truly spectacular specimen to be a Cameron Jr. Lesser penises have begged for the name and been denied. He's a legend unto himself. He stands to attention and other penises salute him."

Angel covered my mouth. "Stop talking about your penis, or I'm going to whip out my vagina and show it to you."

I screeched in disgust. "Don't threaten me with such horrors!"

"Penis," says a small voice from the backseat.

Angel turned around and giggled. "Someone is awake now."

My three-year-old daughter giggled and started singing "penis" over and over as Angel continued laughing uncontrollably. I cringed and called out, "Addy baby, please don't tell Daddy Gavin that I taught you to say penis. Blame it on Angel."

She continued singing the word and made it even catchy sounding. Angel and I sang the word with her. When we pulled up to the pick-up lane at the airport, I got out to give Gavin an appropriate kiss while Angel distracted our daughter from seeing him. Gavin snuck around the side of the car, and the moment Addy spotted him, she screeched, "Daddy Gavin!" which came out sounding almost perfect, with still a little toddler twist to it.

Gavin planted kisses all over her face and said, "I missed you, Addy-bug."

She giggled and said, "Penis!" to which Gavin glanced up to see Angel and me both biting our lips to hold back laughter.

I thought Gavin would laugh, but instead, he looked worried. "Baby girl, please don't say that word."

Angel and I exchanged a look, and she jumped from the front seat and slid into the back next to Addy. "Gavin, sit up front with your husband, and I will entertain my niece."

Angel kept Addy distracted as we drove, and she didn't utter the word again for the ride home. Once we arrived, Angel took Addy inside while I pulled Gavin aside to talk. "It was an accident she heard the word. Addy was sound asleep, and Angel and I were being silly."

Gavin closed his eyes and said, "You have to be careful what you say around a three-year-old, they repeat everything."

"I know. At least it wasn't a curse word. I'm not a terrible father for teaching her anatomical words, right?" Angel and I should've been speaking more child-friendly, but in our defense, Addy can sleep through everything so I never thought she'd hear us.

"I wish she hadn't learned that particular word yet. Not when…" His words trailed off, and he turned to grab his luggage, attempting to avoid dwelling on it further.

"Not when, what?" I pressed.

He dropped the luggage and angrily replied, "Not when we're two gay men raising a daughter and people already think we're pedophiles."

"You worry about other people too much."

Gavin became angrier than I'd ever seen, his face reddened, his teeth clenched. "I worry about people taking our daughter away from us! I worry about people thinking we're hurting her in unspeakable ways because of how they feel about our lifestyle. I worry about you because you come home covered in bruises disguised with makeup and expect me not to notice you've been beaten up."

"You knew?"

"Of course, I knew! I didn't say anything because I wanted you to want to tell me. I know it had to be an act of homophobic bigotry or you'd have told me immediately." Gavin reached forward and pressed his hands against my face, his eyes glistening with tears ready to spill over. "I understand you want to protect me, but you and Addy are my whole life. Without either of you, I'm nothing. I'm terrified of losing you both because of the hatred in this world." He leaned his forehead against mine, and by that time, we were both in tears.

"I'm not going anywhere, and I will die before I let them take Addy away from us. I'm sorry. I'll do better, I'll be more careful." Comedy had been my way to deal with everything, but I needed to grow up. The people in my life must be protected at all costs.

Gavin pulled me into his tight embrace and held me close. I felt his nose against my hair as he breathed. He pressed his lips against my neck and whispered, "I missed you so much."

"I missed you too. I'm sorry I didn't tell you about the attack. I didn't want to worry you." Our lips met with a frantic kiss of emotions. Pent up anger, the loneliness from being apart, the love we shared, everything spilled out in one mind-blowing kiss.

Gavin forced me to look him in the eyes. "From now on, tell me everything. I worry more when I don't know what's happening. Where did you get attacked?"

I spilled everything to Gavin about the attack outside the club. His emotions were all over the place as he teetered between anger and despair. He cried on my shoulder until Angel stepped outside and called our names. "What happened?" she asked when she saw Gavin's face.

I stepped forward to give him a chance to gather himself before we went inside. "I told him about the attack."

Angel eyed Gavin sympathetically. "I'm sorry we lied to you."

Gavin hugged her, taking Angel by surprise. "Thank you for taking care of my better half."

"Only repaying the favor for the many times he's taken care of me," Angel replied with a sympathetic smile.

FOURTEEN

ANGEL

When my phone rang, I almost didn't answer because it was an unknown number. "*Hola, esto es Angel,*" I said with my best Spanish accent.

"*Hola, hermosa, es Marcus. El acento español es caliente,*" Marcus replied without skipping a beat. At the end, he rolled his *r*'s in a sexy growl causing my knees to weaken. "My Spanish is a little limited, so I hope we can speak in English from this point on."

"How limited is it?"

"I know enough words to get me laid in pretty much any language," Marcus replied honestly. "Though German isn't really the sexiest language, so I don't use it too often."

"At least you're honest about it. So, you're trying to get laid?"

Suddenly he seemed nervous. "No, I mean, I want to get to know you. It's not about getting laid. Don't get me wrong, I'd love to have you in my bed, but it's not the only goal I have. You know, I'm going to stop talking. Are you busy?"

I laughed because his honesty was so refreshing I found it appealing. "If you call binge-watching *Grey's Anatomy* as busy, then yes. McDreamy and I have been hanging out all morning."

I had been having a streak of good days on my meds with no pain or weakness. It seemed too good to be true, and I had been running myself ragged while I had the chance. Because of that, I took the day off to rest as much as possible.

"Are you up to the seasons with that Callie chick? She's hot. I kind of have a thing for Hispanic women."

"Oh really?" I inquired with a grin. I curled my feet up under the comforter and put my head back on my pillows. "Yep, she's dating Arizona now. Their scenes are pretty steamy."

"No doubt. By the way, I hope it's okay I got your number from Cameron."

I'd given Cameron hell about giving out my number, but the smile on my face when I heard Marcus's voice was undeniable. I owed Cameron a big one.

"Of course, I'm glad you did. I didn't mean to act weird after our make-out session. It took me by surprise, that's all." Even though it'd been two weeks since we'd seen each other, the smell of his skin, the taste of him, was still fresh in my mind. Talking to him, feeling the effect on my body, the way my heart beat faster and my grin grew wider, I wondered if this was how it felt to fall in love.

"No need to apologize. The reason I was calling is because of the make-out session. You're an amazing kisser, Miss Angel. I wanted the chance to experience it again, after a real date. I'd like to wine and dine you and see what we have in common."

"I don't drink wine."

"You dine though, right?" Marcus remarked.

"I'm not sure it's a good idea for us to date." My arch nemesis alcohol always reared its ugly face when it came to Marcus. Perhaps it was a sign he was too much temptation.

"What can I do to convince you otherwise?" Marcus was a man on a mission and he wasn't going to give up easily, the way I hoped he would. When I didn't respond, he found his own way to be convincing. He lowered his voice to a seductive tone. "I know you wanted me as much as I wanted you, Angel. I felt the heat coming off your body. You thrusting against me made me so rock hard I could barely walk the rest of the evening."

I gulped and bit my lip as I remembered how good he felt on top of me. "It was nice."

Marcus grew silent. A moment later, he spat, "Nice? Seriously you're going with nice? You're a mean woman."

"Okay, I'll admit, it was a hot make-out session." Hot was putting it mildly, but he wasn't getting more from me.

"I have an idea. If I can prove a statement, will you go out with me?"

"What statement?" I asked, admittedly intrigued.

"I can make you reach orgasm over the phone without ever touching yourself."

I choked on air at the unexpected turn of events. "Seeing as how it takes a lot for a man to make me orgasm with sex, I take the challenge. If you can do it, I'll go to dinner with you. Dinner is all I'm promising." Taking things slowly got thrown out the window with his new challenge. Intrigued by his claim, I had to see if he could live up to his word.

"Deal. You have to promise to do everything I tell you. Are you ready?"

"Yep. Your wish is my command." Sex had never made me nervous. In my past, I frequently made the first move. With Marcus not even in the room, it was the safest sex possible too.

"Do you have a ceiling fan?" was the first question Marcus asked.

Glancing above me at the fan I rarely ever used, I replied. "Yes."

"Perfect. Turn on the ceiling fan and then take off all of your clothes."

"I'll freeze!" I exclaimed.

"Trust me, you won't," he promised.

Shuffling to the door, I flipped the light switch connected to the fan. "Ceiling fan is on." My hips shimmied until my panties fell to the floor, and then I removed my T-shirt and tossed it across the room. "Clothes are off."

Marcus sucked in a breath. "Maybe we should FaceTime this."

I chuckled. "You wish."

"A guy can try. Now lie down on your back. Place your hands next to you with palms down. Spread your feet until they are lined with the bedposts, exposing yourself as much as possible."

In order to place my hands next to me, I had to put him on speakerphone. I set the phone next to my head and assumed the position. "Done, you better hurry up and get me warm." My teeth chattered as the cold air lapped at my body from above. Admittedly, his voice alone had begun to affect me.

"Shh. Listen." His voice became sensual and deep. "Close your eyes. Do you feel the air from the fan?"

"Yes, and my nipples could cut glass." A low soft chuckle from him sent tingles across my skin.

"I'm at the edge of the bed. You can feel my warm breath against your skin. Starting at your ankles, I trail kisses up your calves pushing your legs open as I move further up the bed." As he spoke the words, I imagined his touch to the point of feeling the wet trail from his lips. I opened an eye to make sure he wasn't there.

"Keep your eyes closed," he said making me shut my eye again. The way he knew I peeked creeped me out a little.

"Feel the air from the ceiling fan lapping at your body? Now it's my tongue mimicking the movements of the fan as it circles your clit." With each word, I grew warmer and wetter.

I bucked my hips off the bed as I felt a surge of passion course through me. I gasped and sat up. "Wait." I jumped up off the bed and ran to check the hallway. No one was out there, so I locked the door and reclaimed my position on the bed; on my back, palms down, feet spread.

"Did you go back to the same position automatically?"

"Yes," I replied, slightly confused.

"See the control I have over you right now? Close your eyes again and let me continue exploring your core." Tingles coursed across my skin as I once again could feel his mouth and tongue exploring my body. Imagination was a wonderful thing.

He continued explaining every movement he made, each swirl of the tongue, every nibble along the way. Describing how I tasted on his tongue, the softness of my body, I'd swear he was there with me. Not once had I touched myself, though he certainly made it difficult not to. I began to think he had been a little too cocky when suddenly my body quivered, and a jolt lifted me from the bed as the convulsions rocked me. I gasped out his name without a thought and clapped my hand over my mouth.

"I… what just happened?" I asked, wiping the sweat from my forehead.

"I brought you to orgasm without anyone touching you. What did you think?"

"I'm free for dinner whenever you are," I said, sighing with delight at the shudders still coursing over my skin.

FIFTEEN

CAMERON

"**S**hut up! Over the phone, and you never once strummed the banjo?" I exclaimed as Angel told me about her dirty phone session with Marcus.

"Not even once. My hands stayed next to me. So now we have a date tomorrow night." Raising my hand in the air, I brought it down to my shoulder giving myself a hearty pat on the back for excellent matchmaking skills.

"A *date*? Hell, I'd be proposing marriage!" I shrieked into the phone.

"Let me get through a date or two first," Angel teased. "Did you tell Marcus I'm an alcoholic?"

"I'm not one who goes around telling people's business, Angel. You should be the one to tell him when you're ready." Granted, I had informed him of her MS, but I felt it was a need to know. He needed to know she was vulnerable and not to hurt her. I hoped she wouldn't wait too long to tell him about the alcoholism. It shouldn't change his view of her, but it made a difference on what he planned for them.

"Ok, good. It just seems odd because every time I offer him a drink, he assumes I mean alcohol."

I chuckled softly. "Occupational hazard, he's a bartender. He's not a jerk. I can vouch for him there. And if he knew he would be a jerk to assume a recovering alcoholic would offer liquor."

Marcus had secrets of his own, and I wouldn't share those with Angel. I didn't know of anything which would affect her negatively or I'd tell her about it. The two had a similar upbringing and experienced many of the same heartaches in life. Marcus hadn't been raped, but he'd been abused heavily by his stepfather. Both of them had trust issues and both had a large number of notches on their bedposts.

"Call me after your date. I'm going to want all the details."

"Details about what?" came a voice from behind me. I hung up the phone and spun around on my heels about falling over in fright.

"What the hell, Gracie! You scared the shit out of me. How did you get in here?" I had been at the club this morning working on new design concepts for the interior. When we bought the building, there was a large room off the back we planned to use for extra storage if needed. We'd found we didn't need it so now they wanted to design another private party room since our calendar was booked solid.

"I have a key, silly." Gracie stepped forward looking concerned as I held my chest to keep my heart from beating completely out of it. "Cam, you're really scared," she commented after she placed her hand over my heart. "Do you want to talk?"

"What are you doing here?" I asked, annoyed at myself. Bigoted homophobes had made me afraid of my own shadow. After the attack, Marcus had offered to ride into work with me each day, promising he'd use car troubles as an excuse. I considered the offer but decided I couldn't let myself live in fear. Perhaps I was wrong thinking I could do it on my own.

Gracie's face softened into sadness. She peered down at her hands in a shy manner and whispered, "I've missed you."

I wrapped my arms around her. "I'm sorry, baby girl. I'm not mad at you, only myself for being a chicken shit. You look fabulous, motherhood definitely agrees with you."

"Thanks, Cam. Ash is taking care of Autumn, and I took time off work. I was hoping to spend it with my best friend, if he'll have me."

My face lit up, and I lifted Gracie in a bear hug and spun her once. Before Ashton and Gavin were in the picture, we spent almost every waking minute together. Since we married our loves, we'd barely spent more than a few hours together a month.

"Are we hanging out here?"

"I had different plans for us. Gavin is aware of my plans and is taking care of Addy. In fact, he's hanging out with Ash and Autumn.

I want us to have a pampering day like old times. It's my treat, for a change, since I have the money to do so." I started to argue when she held up her hand and continued her thought. "No arguing with me, Cam. I'm buying. When I was in college you treated me to everything, even helped me pay rent a few times. Let me spoil you. After pedicures and wraps at the spa, we'll go to the winery for a tasting, and at the end of the night, Angel and MJ will meet us for dinner and gossip."

"How did you know I needed this time with you?"

Gracie shrugged her shoulders with a lopsided grin. "I'm a smart girl. Plus, I've missed you, and I selfishly want to have things be like old times between us for at least a day."

The spa we chose was located on the outskirts of Nashville in Franklin. We began with a couple's massage so we could talk while relaxing. Gracie's masseuse was a petite woman with muscular arms and hot pink hair tied into a bun on top of her head. My stud muffin was a beautiful specimen of man with a slick bald head and dark chocolate skin.

Talking from the side of my mouth, I lowered my voice and said, "Holy hotness Batman, am I the only one hearing seventies porn music in my head right now?"

Gracie skimmed her eyes over my masseuse and her lips formed into an O as she scoped him out from abs to ass. She gave me thumbs up and a low, "bow-chick-a-wow wow. OW!" The last syllable came out in a scream of pain as the now nightmare with pink hair dug her elbow into Gracie's back.

"What the fuck, Helga! You're supposed to make her relaxed, not put her in traction!" Her name wasn't Helga, but she acted like you'd expect a Helga to act. Gracie had tears in her eyes. I jumped up with Cameron Jr at full attention and reached out for Gracie. "Are you okay?"

"Yes, my shoulder has been bothering me for a while. Ashton has been begging me to get it looked at, but I've put it off." She rolled over and made eye contact with the vicious torturer standing to the right. "I'm sorry he freaked out on you, he worries about me." Gracie grabbed the towel covering her and twisted into a seated position. "I think I'll go get my pedicure now." Stretching her back, she cringed again.

"I'm going to let LL Cool Hands finish me off… my massage I mean. No happy endings for this married fellow." Gracie chuckled at me as she padded out of the room in her terrycloth slippers.

A half-hour later, I sat next to Gracie with my feet in a tub of warm water. "Talk to me, Gracie. How are things with your hunk of a husband?"

"Things are perfect, Ash is amazing. When Autumn was born, we got into a bit of a sexual rut, but he bought us a book on sex positions, and we've been trying a new one each week. It's really livened up our sex life again."

"You slut, so we know why your shoulder is sore! Fess up, what's been your favorite position?" I sat up and rested my chin on my hand waiting intently for the details.

"One called the pretzel. It's exactly how it sounds too. But oh my gosh, the orgasm was so intense I fell off the bed the first time we did it. Now we surround ourselves with pillows." Gracie licked her lips and laid her head back letting out an exaggerated sigh.

"Calm yourself, girlfriend, don't go all Meg Ryan in *When Harry Met Sally* on me." Today had been exactly what I needed, a day of fun with my bestie. She'd be angry with me if she found out about my attack. I hadn't told her because she always had so much going on, she didn't need to worry about me as well.

After our spa day ended, Gracie drove us to the restaurant to meet the other girls. Walking up to the table, I exclaimed, "Girls day out! Who's ordering the margaritas?"

Mary Jane scrunched her face up. "I can't drink because I have to pick up Craig and Katelyn from Maria's after this. Derrick's at the club tonight."

Angel cocked her head to the side. "I can't drink while I'm an alcoholic."

Gracie peered over at me and shrugged. "I'm supporting my girls."

"Is this what growing up feels like? Because, pardon the pun, it's very sobering." Taking my seat, I waved the waiter over and ordered. "I'll take a virgin rum and coke please." Noticing the confused look on the face of the poor guy, I clarified, "I want a Coke, sweetie."

"So, Angel McMuffin, did you tell these ladies about your

sexcapades with a ceiling fan?" I loved watching her face as she choked down the drink of water and her eyes bulged out.

Gracie and Mary Jane turned in their chairs to face Angel. "Do tell us." Gracie leaned forward with her head resting on her hand. Mary Jane scooted closer to hear each detail. After Angel went through the entire story again, we were all fanning ourselves in awe of Marcus.

"We're going out tomorrow night. I want to take things slow, but after that, I'm dying to know what it's like when he's in bed *with* me!" A round of high fives followed by laughter filled the table. Who needed alcohol to have a good time? Not our group for sure.

SIXTEEN

ANGEL

It had been weeks since I'd had a flare up, and this morning I woke up in pain. The night was finally here, I was supposed to go on a date with Marcus, and I'd picked up the phone six times to cancel. Each time I stopped myself as I considered how anxious I'd been to see him since our call a few nights before. Orgasm or not, the laughter made me want to see him. No man, other than Cameron, had made me smile or laugh as much as he did. Tasting happiness made me crave it even more.

Since I'd gotten out of rehab, I'd kept my pain pills locked up so I wouldn't overuse them. I pulled them down and took a dose, chasing them with a gulp of water. "Angel," Macy called as she knocked on my door.

Slipping inside my room, her face scrunched up when she saw me wincing. "I'm fine, sweetie. Come on in. You can help me get ready."

"Tristan said you had a date tonight. Marcus from the bar?" I nodded. "He's hot," she said with a blush filling her cheeks.

"He sure is. Would you mind picking out my outfit for me?" Macy sprinted toward the closet, giving me a chance to let the pain ease off. If I quelled the pain enough to a tolerable level, I would make it through the night, and Marcus would never know anything was wrong.

Appearing a few minutes later, Macy held up a black shirt, sleeveless on one side and lined with beads along the neck to go with a pair of white jeans. After laying those on the bed, she grabbed a pair of black boots from the closet and matching jewelry out of my case. As I strained to brush my hair, she gently placed her hand on mine and took the brush from me. "I've never had a sister until I met you and MJ. The two of you have done a lot for me. Let me give back a little."

Grinning, I bit my lip to hold back the tears. "Thank you" was all I could say. Flare-ups affected every muscle of my body when they were bad. Even something as simple as brushing my hair was a lot of work. Combing my hair into a twist, she snapped it into place with a barrette, leaving me a nice ponytail hanging down. Medicine had kicked in a bit so I was able to get myself dressed, and then I took a glance in the mirror. "Nice job, Macy."

Smiling, she replied, "I didn't have to do much. You're gorgeous." Squeezing her in my arms, I hoped that if I ever had a daughter one day, she'd be like Macy.

Interrupted by the doorbell, Macy's eyebrows rose as her eyes widened. "Are you ready?"

Taking a deep breath, I felt like a teenager on prom night. "Let's do this."

Macy ran ahead of me to grab the door, and I heard her giggling with Marcus as I came down the stairs. Dressed in a dark maroon button-down shirt with black slacks, he looked good enough to eat. Licking my lips, I imagined him doing things to me he'd described on the phone the other night. When his gaze drifted over to me, his eyes lit up and his mouth fell open. In his hands, he held a single red rose. Taking the last step, Marcus reached out for my hand and helped me down. "You're smokin' hot." I snorted with laughter as I expected something different.

"Bring her back by eleven. She has a curfew," Macy said, throwing me a wink. Marcus kissed her cheek and then escorted me out the door.

In a gentlemanly move, he opened the car door for me, and once I slipped inside, he sprinted around the car to get in. He buckled and turned to face me. "I'm not used to being Mr. Romance. So if I'm overdoing it or being cheesy, please tell me."

Sliding my fingers across his hand, I said, "Just be yourself. That's the person I agreed to go out with." It seemed a good time to fill him in on one part of my baggage before we ended up somewhere uncomfortable for me. "There's something I should tell you before we go." Marcus curled his lips up and squinted his eyes. "I'm a recovering alcoholic."

His features relaxed, and you could almost see the light come on above his head. "Explains a lot really. You always get so offended by the mention of alcohol. I thought maybe you were uber religious or something."

"It's not a problem for you?"

"Nope. As long as my job isn't a problem for you." I shook my head. "I have a favorite restaurant I'd like to take you to. Do you like Italian food?"

"Sure. I'll pretty much eat anything." A weight lifted from my shoulders when he blew off my confession with ease. If he could handle my baggage so easily, he had to be something special.

Turns out, the restaurant was only a few minutes from my house. Marcus had the car valet parked and extended his arm to lead me inside. Still working on the romance angle, he pulled the chair out for me before taking his own seat.

Silently reading over the menu, we each placed our order and sat fidgeting nervously. Each time we'd met, we'd been able to joke around or tease each other; suddenly we were like two people on a blind date with nothing to talk about.

"So what is the likelihood of me getting laid tonight? Because that could totally affect how much I'm willing to spend on this meal."

"What the fuck?" I asked, appalled at how wrong I'd been about this guy.

Grinning mischievously, Marcus winked. "Just trying to break the ice."

"You almost made me break your face."

Setting his menu down, he slid his hand over mine. "It's been a long time since I wanted to sit and listen to a woman talk. I want to know more about you than what you look like naked." Licking his lips, he added, "Don't get me wrong, I do want to know that too."

Lips sucked in, I tried to hold back the smile. "For now, what would you like me to talk about?"

"How long have you been in recovery?" His first question went deeper than I expected. Obviously sensing my discomfort, he said, "I've been sober six months."

"But you work at a bar?"

"Amazingly enough, I want it less since I started working around it. Watching people get drunk off their asses and make a complete fool of themselves is high motivation for not drinking. I'm ashamed to admit it, but I've been with women who I couldn't even remember the next day because I met them when I was wasted." Marcus might as well have been telling my story. We were more alike than I knew.

"Did Cameron tell you anything about me?" Emotional walls were being constructed as I began to wonder if I was being played because he knew my story.

"Besides your phone number, the only thing Cameron said is he loves the hell out of you and will root for us, but I had to get any other information directly from you." Truth resonated in his eyes, and the words were definitely Cameron's.

"Men sleeping around are players, but I've been in your situation and most consider me a slut." The double standard was nothing new for me. I'd been called a whore and every other synonym for the word.

"I'd fight anyone who tried to call you a slut. And I know the rest of your friends would too. You're a goddess. I'm not feeding you a line. I've been admiring you from afar for a while now." The sincerity in his eyes was undeniable.

Naughty Angel wanted to forget about dinner and take Marcus back to his place to do a variety of dirty things. Ten things came to mind about his lips alone. Reformed Angel had me crossing my legs tighter as I tried to get to know him on a more permanent level. A quickie in the backseat wouldn't be enough with this man. Once we got started, I had a feeling fireworks would ensue and I'd want a few encore sessions at least.

"What nefarious plans are you coming up with over there?"

"I've been sober a year. And if you had met me a year ago, we'd already be in the car with my legs wrapped around your neck."

Marcus choked on the sip of water he'd attempted to swallow just now. "Where's a freaking time machine when you need one?" he joked once he could speak again. Having a good laugh at his joke, I almost felt guilty for teasing him. The way the night was going, I may not be able to stick to my no sex idea.

For the next hour, we talked about our personal lives. Marcus had six sisters; he'd told me about them before. He only saw them on holidays when he could afford to fly home. Our families were a lot alike, though I only had two brothers. We were both holiday family people and spent more time with friends than anything. Then there was the alcohol issue. For him, the drinking began in high school shortly after his dad died. His mother remarried within a year. His stepfather took everything out on Marcus. He took the beatings, grateful the man wasn't beating his mother instead. He drank to numb the pain the first time he suffered a broken bone. I blamed mine on loneliness. It seemed like a lot of baggage to lay my illness on him at this point.

When the check came, I tried to pay, but Marcus snatched it from me. Reaching out he took my hand and led me to the valet station. "It may sound weird, but would you want to go dancing at A Shot in the Dark tonight?"

"I haven't found a way to deal with the temptation as easily as you have yet. There's a lot of alcohol there to lure me into its dark shadows." Hoards of people on the dance floor with drinks in their hands seemed like the worst possible position to put myself in. Then again, if I avoided it forever, I'd never know my own strength. "If I can't handle it, we may have to leave early."

Leaning over he whispered in my ear, "We'll only stay as long as you're comfortable." Shivers of pleasure flowed over my skin with the feel of his breath on my neck. Biting my lip, I found I couldn't say no to this man.

The valet arrived with our car and held the door open for me as Marcus sprinted around to the driver's seat. Music played softly in the car, and I watched as Marcus sang along. My eyes traced over his strong jawline, over his supple lips, and down to his thick neck. Desire washed over me, and I leaned over to press a lingering kiss against his cheek. Coming to a stop at the red light, Marcus turned and captured my lips with his. His hands pushed through my hair as his tongue slid into my mouth. My hand slipped inside his shirt, sliding over the smooth muscle beneath.

Horns honked as the light turned green. Marcus turned his attention back to the road as I moved up to his ear, biting the lobe. "Damn, Angel. You're making things very hard for me right now."

Boldly going where I didn't plan to go, I straddled his waist once the car was parked at the club. Our tongues moved together rhythmically, and I gasped when I felt his hand pressed against my core, rubbing me through my tight jeans.

Resisting alcohol seemed like a breeze in comparison to resisting Marcus. I'd gone a year without a man in my bed, and since the moment I met him, I couldn't stop wondering what it would be like to be with him. As much as I fought my old ways, they continued to work against me.

Grinding against his hand, I could feel my release building. Damn this man and his super orgasm abilities. He dropped the driver's seat back, and I fell forward. His hand slipped down the front of my pants, and it took three strokes against my clit before I came in a powerful quiver above him.

Rolling over to the passenger side again, I panted, "I didn't mean for that to happen."

"I'm not complaining."

"I guess I need to do something for you now." I propped up on my knees ready to service him the way I'd done men in the past. Marcus surprised me when he placed his hand out to cover his zipper.

"Tonight's all about you. You can do for me another time."

While he walked around the car to open my door, I sat stunned. No guy, before Marcus, had given me an orgasm outside of sex for one thing, and no man had ever pleasured me without demanding some in return. Some took what they wanted whether I offered it or not. Sadly, it was the life I'd become accustomed to leading.

"Come on, beautiful. I want to see your dance moves." Taking his hand, I followed him to the door. "Bobby, my man!" Marcus held up a high five to the bouncer. "Busy night?"

Bobby replied, "Full house." He tipped his head toward me. "Good to see you again, Ms. Angel."

Bobby had always been a sweet southern gentleman to me. If he hadn't been into guys, I'd have asked him out a long time ago. "Hey, sweet cheeks." Giving him a kiss on the cheek, I hugged him tight before slipping inside.

The room was filled with bodies gyrating to the latest music. Marcus dragged me to the dance floor bypassing the bar completely. I caught Tristan's eye and waved at him. Circling behind me, Marcus pulled me against him, my back to his front. He pressed his lips against my bare shoulder, gently nibbling on my skin. Excitement from our rendezvous in the car was still evident in his pants, so I decided to give a little back. Rotating my hips, I bumped my butt against him, sliding down his body and back up again. Marcus's hands were on my sides, and he held on following each movement, fully clothed we drove each other to ecstasy. Turning his back to the crowd, he had me face the wall so we couldn't be seen. He slipped his hand across my chest sliding beneath the hem, tweaking a nipple with his thumb and forefinger.

Still moving against him in a dance of seduction, I felt his hand graze down my stomach. No doubt loving the personal attention, I needed him now. The whole concept of waiting was thrown out the door and kicked down the street. Dragging him through the crowd to the office in the back, we fell through the doorway. Luckily Cameron wasn't utilizing his office right then. Locking the door behind me, I flung myself at Marcus kissing him as I pushed him toward the couch. Flinging off my shirt, I sucked in a breath when his teeth found my pert nipples.

As I fell to the couch, he landed on top of me devouring my mouth as we worked to remove our clothes. All the frantic movements and stretching of the past few hours was taking a toll on me. The pain meds were wearing off and the muscle pain had crept back. I cringed in pain, trying to hide my face from Marcus.

Resting above me now, wearing a pair of damn sexy pale grey boxer briefs with a sizeable bulge, he stopped. "I can't do this."

"What?" I panted. "Why?" Had he seen the pain in my eyes? How would I explain why I hadn't told him about it already? How much baggage can I lay on someone during a first date without scaring them away entirely?

Gathering up his clothes, he said, "I'm sorry, Angel. Can you get a ride home tonight? I have to go." And a moment later, he was out the door still buttoning his shirt. The door opened, and I jumped to cover myself when I saw Cameron's face.

SEVENTEEN

CAMERON

Glancing back out the door, I saw Marcus leaving disheveled, and I turned to see Angel sitting topless on my couch. I closed and locked the door behind me, picked her shirt up, and handed it to her. "Tell me he hurt you and I'll go kick his ass right now." From what I knew of Marcus, it seemed unlikely he would do anything to Angel, but then again people have shocked me before.

"I... I don't know what happened. We were having an amazing date and we agreed to take it slowly, which lasted about two seconds. Next thing I knew, I was jumping his bones in the car, and then we almost had sex on your dancefloor before coming in here. He was practically naked before he stopped without explanation." Her shirt remained in her hand, a confused look on her face as if she were replaying the events in her mind. Maybe she was. Maybe she thought she had done something wrong.

"Want me to talk to him?" I asked. Marcus had a lot going on lately, and I had a feeling I knew the reason he stopped, but it wasn't my place to tell Angel. Whatever happened tonight had thrown her for a loop. Speechless wasn't a way to describe Angel, ever. Her sitting there with a blank look on her face, still topless, disturbed me.

"I'm humiliated enough as it is. I threw myself at him after admitting what a slut I've always been." Frustrated, she jerked the shirt over her head.

"Don't call yourself those kinds of names. You're too hard on yourself. I'm sure Marcus had a good excuse for what happened. Give him a chance to explain." Her eyes were welling up with tears, so I pulled her into an embrace for comfort. *Damn Marcus for hurting my girl.*

"Doesn't matter. Can you take me home? I'm too close to wanting a drink right now." Handing Angel a glass of water, I watched as her hands trembled. "This isn't the drink I want."

Rolling my eyes, I teased, "Gee I had no idea. Just drink the damn thing." Emptying the glass, she handed it back to me. "I'm headed out for the night. You're coming to my house." I wished finding love didn't involve going through hell to get there. With all three of my girls, they suffered great heartache before finding their happiness. Gracie went through something no woman ever should, but in the end, she found everything she wanted in Ashton. Mary Jane's heartache came from leaving Derrick behind while pursuing her dreams. I wanted this to be an easier ride for Angel since she'd already been through hell two or three times in her life.

"Cam... I—"

Hand in the air, I interjected, "No arguing. Get up and let's go."

Neither of us spoke on the drive to my house. My text tone had sounded several times along the way and I was finally able to look when I put the car in park.

Marcus: I need to talk, Cameron. I screwed things up with Angel.

Marcus: Please give me a call. I know she's probably talked to you by now and I need someone to help me explain to her.

Before he could send a third text, I responded.

Me: She's with me. I'll have to call you later. She's my priority right now.

Marcus: Take care of her. I think I screwed up the best chance I had at happiness.

Angel had been quiet while I was texting. Glancing up, I noticed her staring at me. "Is that Gavin?" My hesitation answered her question. "Oh."

Inside, the house was dark and quiet. Gavin and Addison were sound asleep as usual when I came home from the club. "Stay here, I'm going to let Gavin know I'm home, and then we'll talk."

Tiptoeing into the bedroom, I quietly closed the door behind me. Gavin was sound asleep with his mouth hanging open, a tiny bit of drool at the corner, and snoring like a chainsaw. Damn the man was adorable. Pressing my lips to his forehead, he stirred awake. Rubbing his eyes, he sat up. "Hey, baby."

"Shh. Don't get up. Angel is here. She had a rough night and is feeling tempted to drink so I'm going to sit up with her a while. Just wanted to let you know I'm home. I love you." Running my hands through his hair, I pulled him in for a long kiss, not caring about stale breath or drool, only getting a taste of my love.

"Give Angel my love. If you guys need me, wake me up." One more taste of his lips and I let Gavin roll back over to sleep. Screw the world and their views; our love was beautiful.

Before heading back to Angel, I checked in on Addison to be sure she was sleeping soundly. My perfect daughter was peacefully asleep, sucking on her thumb with her tiny hand in a fist.

Back in the living room, Angel sat staring at a bottle of Vodka in our cabinet. Thankfully, Gavin childproofed the entire apartment, which included putting locks on any medicine or alcohol cabinets. "If you think it's worth throwing away how hard you've worked this past year to stay sober, I'll get the key for the cabinet right now."

Whipping around, shock filled Angel's face as the tears clouded her eyes. "Don't tempt me, Cam. I'm not as strong as I once was. The old me would never let a man get close enough to hurt me the way Marcus did."

"My offer still stands because I know you don't want to drink.

You're one of the strongest women I've ever known. You've been to hell and back, and you keep your head high." All my words were honest and true. Never had I known anyone to survive as much crap as Angel and come out standing tall.

"What did he say?" It came out as a whisper, with a quiver in her voice.

"Who? Gavin?" Cocking an eyebrow, she placed her hand on her hip. "Oh. You mean Marcus?" She nodded, so I handed her my phone to see the texts herself.

"Do you know why he stopped?" Trailing her fingers over the screen, she kept her eyes on the message.

"I have an idea. But why don't you call him?" Any reason Marcus had was his to tell, I couldn't betray his confidence by spilling any secrets he'd told me.

Handing my phone back, she pulled hers out of her back pocket. "Hi. Can you meet me tomorrow? I need to talk. I almost drank tonight." She focused her eyes on the ceiling and twirled her hair around her fingers. "Great, I'll see you then."

"So you're meeting Marcus tomorrow?"

"No. I called Gus. As far as Marcus goes, I'm going to wait for him to call me." Knowing how stubborn she was there was no point in arguing the point any further. And I could drop a little hint to Marcus that she would be waiting for his call. "I'm tired. Do you mind if I sleep on your couch?"

"Of course not. I'll grab you some pillows and a blanket." In the hallway closet, we kept spare blankets and a few pillows, so I didn't have to tiptoe too much to set Angel up. Curled up on the couch almost in a fetal position she appeared so fragile. At work, before his shift in the evening, I planned to talk to Marcus and make sure things got worked out. Angel wasn't one to easily fall for someone. I knew this devastation was in part due to her self-loathing in assuming things would never work out for her.

As much as I wanted to curl up in bed next to my husband, I needed to be sure Angel stayed sober. The alcohol was locked up, but I wanted to make sure she slept. I watched from the recliner across from the couch until she drifted off to sleep.

EIGHTEEN

ANGEL

With a smile on his face and a bouquet of daisies, Gus stood outside my door after ringing the bell. "Good morning, beautiful," Gus greeted me through the screen door when he spotted me coming down the stairs.

"Come on in, handsome. You don't have to ring the bell." As soon as he stepped in the door, I wrapped my arms around him and squeezed tightly. "I've missed you," I whispered against his neck.

"Let's sit and talk, sweetheart." Guiding Gus to the couch, I took a seat positioning myself against him. His arm fell across my shoulders, hugging me close. "Tell me what triggered the need for you last night."

I took a deep breath and released it slowly, stalling as long as I could to keep from reliving my embarrassment. In the meantime,

Gus patiently waited for me to answer. Occasionally he kissed my forehead or squeezed my shoulder as a reminder he was still there. I loved Gus. In the short time we'd been friends, he'd been the best at helping me maintain my sobriety. He had a way of calming me like no one else could. Life would be so much easier if he and I were attracted to one another romantically.

"If it keeps you from drinking, we'll sit here in silence for as long as you need." After another few moments of quiet, he cleared his throat. "I wanted to drink about two weeks ago." I glanced up at him in shock, wondering why he hadn't told me before. After rehab, we'd promised to sponsor each other for life. "Yep. Drove to the store, bought a bottle of whiskey, and poured myself a glass, on the rocks. You know what stopped me?" I shook my head. "Mike."

"How?"

"I was in a bad place, Angel. My life seemed to be going nowhere, and I have no one." I opened my mouth to speak when he leaned his forehead against mine. "Darlin', you know I don't mean you. I mean romantically. Everything seemed to be falling in around me, and it hit me all at once. The moment I poured the drink, I heard Mike say, 'Ain't happenin', Gus,' just like he used to." My chest tightened. I heard Mike's voice as clear as day through Gus. "And after I heard his voice in my head, I looked over and saw the picture of the three of us from our final day in rehab."

"Why didn't you call me?"

"I broke down crying and had a long talk with Mike. It helped to hear myself admit the things in my life bringing me down. I actually looked in the mirror, told myself to stop being such a pussy, and start living life to honor Mike. Remember he asked us in his letter to do a few things for him?" In Mike's suicide note, he had made us promise to take a trip for him. He'd been cremated, and with no family, his remains went to Gus. He wanted his remains sprinkled in the mountains of Gatlinburg, Tennessee, the last vacation he had with his wife, the place where they married. Neither of us had been ready for honoring his request until now. It seemed the perfect time.

"Let's take the trip next weekend."

"Sounds great, but first I need you to tell me what happened last night."

For a moment, I'd forgotten the reason for Gus's visit. One thing was for sure, I needed to make a better effort to see him on a regular basis. "Marcus and I went on a date last night, and I made an immense fool of myself. The worst part is I really like him, and he ran away from me as though the thought of sleeping me was the most disgusting idea on the planet."

"On behalf of all men, he would be an idiot to think anything about you was disgusting. So what's wrong with him? Impotent maybe?"

Snorting in laughter, I kissed Gus's cheek. "If he's impotent, he carries a bat in his pocket."

"A bat? Seriously?" Gus glanced down at his crotch pushing his bottom lip out in a pout. I chuckled as I patted his leg.

"Gus-Gus, how do I fix things with him?"

"Fixing this is not what you need right now. You and I need to attend a meeting. There's one that starts within the hour and it's about a fifteen-minute drive from here. I googled it after you called. It would be helpful for you to sit in on one before you tackle this problem."

Reluctantly I stood up, walked across the room, and grabbed my purse off the hook by the door. "Let's go," I said as I tossed my purse across my shoulder. "Afterward, I'll treat us to dinner at Rotier's."

"Girl, you speak straight to my stomach. Let's go."

Gus was right. The meeting was exactly what I needed. A woman stepped up in front of the room and said, "My name is Karina and I'm an alcoholic." The room erupted with the normal response of "Welcome, Karina." Her lip barely twitched into a smile before she began her story. "My first drink was at the age of thirteen. It would be easy to stand up here and blame it on some tragic event in my life, but the truth is, I was a curious teen. My parents didn't pay much attention to me. They were too busy leaving me with the babysitters and taking long trips without me. My way of punishing them was to drink myself into a stupor every time they were gone. When I was seventeen, my father came home and found me drunk. His response was to pour more liquor and force it down my throat assuming it was my first time and it would make me sick. He didn't know I'd been doing this for so long."

"Jesus," I whispered to Gus. He nodded and squeezed my hand tightly.

"Last year I drove myself head first into a tree. After ten years of drinking nonstop, I was tired of punishing myself. I was in a coma for six months as my body healed from the injuries. When I woke up, even with the court ordered rehab, I had decided I would take charge of my life and make things better. I would stop living in the past and blaming my parents for my problems. I'm taking charge. I'm going after what I want, a job, a family, a normal life." Tears streamed down Karina's face. We were the same age, and she appeared so much wiser than me. In a way, she was telling my story. The words weren't the same, but the moral was.

Leaning over to Gus, I whispered, "Let's leave tomorrow for Gatlinburg. I want to take the trip before I decide anything about my future with Marcus. We need to say our final goodbye to Mike, and I need to say goodbye to my past. Only then can I move on with Marcus"—my voice lowered to a mumble—"if there is a future for us."

"You need to let him know you want to talk." Gus pointed at my phone. I sighed and began to type out a text.

Me: I'd like for us to talk about what happened the other night.

Marcus: I'm free tonight. The sooner, the better.

Me: Not tonight. I'm taking a trip with my friend Gus-Gus. I'll text you in a couple of days so we can meet.

Marcus: Okay, I look forward to it.

NINETEEN

CAMERON

Marcus stormed into my office. "Who's Gus-Gus?"

"The mouse in Cinderella? Jack's friend, chubby little guy." I couldn't help myself. I knew who he was referring to and had to have a little fun at his expense.

"Who is Gus-Gus to Angel?" And it dawned on me; the redness on his face wasn't filled with anger but jealousy. I needed a moment to consider how to explain who Gus was without giving away Angel's stint in rehab. She deserved the chance to tell Marcus about it on her own terms, and I wasn't sure she'd had a chance yet.

"He's a friend, as far as I know. Why?"

"She's going on a trip with him? Should I be jealous?"

"From the looks of it, you already are. After walking out on her the other night though, I'm not sure you have a right to be." His hands shook, his nostrils flared, and I could almost smell the oncoming display of ownership for his woman. "Where are they going?"

"She didn't say. Can you call and ask her? Find out what's happening between them, if I have a chance—"

"Slow down. I'll see what I can find out." Before he had a meltdown, I dialed up my girl to get the scoop. "Hello, gorgeous!"

"Hey, Cam, what's up?"

"What are you up to this weekend? I thought we could hang out." So I told a white lie; it was better than saying her potential man mate was looking rather green.

"I'm going to Gatlinburg with Gus for a couple days. When I get back, we can pick a day to hang. I'd love to go to the zoo with you and Addy."

"Gatlinburg? That's a pretty romantic destination." Peering up, I noticed Marcus's ears perked up like a corgi. And the shade of green washing over him made me chuckle. He had it bad for my girl.

"Gus and I are just friends. You can relay the message to Marcus too."

"What is that supposed to mean?"

"It means, I just texted him to tell him I was going out of town. I know he's at work, and we never make plans ahead of time. You always call and say 'bitch, let's go do something fun now.' So, reassure Marcus, we're going to talk soon." Damn, I loved how smart she was. No one pulled the wool over Angel's eyes; she was on top of it.

"Will do. Have fun on your trip." Before I could end the call, Marcus stomped forward and stopped with his arms crossed over his chest. "Down, boy. She and Gus are friends only. She knew you were the reason I asked, and she said to make sure you understand she still plans to meet up with you when she comes back."

Dropping down to the couch, he placed his feet up on the armrest. He ran his hands through his hair letting out a loud groan. "What the hell is happening to me, Cam? I've never been so whipped by a woman. I'm not a jealous guy."

"They call it love, Marcus. And you're smack dab in the middle of it." I had to admit it made me happy to see my two friends falling for one another. The only problem was they were both miserable and hiding their true feelings. Since I would have a few days with Angel out of town, I planned to use my matchmaking abilities to work on getting him to open up fully to her. "Tomorrow's your day off, right?" Marcus nodded. "Spend the day with me and my daughter. Gavin is working, and I can give you some pointers on what to do with Angel. If you want them."

Those ears perked up again as he sat up straight on the couch. "I do want."

TWENTY

ANGEL

Getting time off work with such short notice wasn't a problem. I'd been picking up several shifts lately for a hairdresser, and she owed me a favor. She wasn't a flake, just a single mom with a sick kid. She was grateful to be able to make up some of the time she'd lost.

Gus picked me up at four o'clock in the morning. He knew better than anyone how little of a morning person I was, but he insisted on an early start. Throwing my hair up in a ponytail, I trudged downstairs in my pajama pants and sweatshirt, grabbing my luggage off the chair. Gus opened the door, I'd left it unlocked for him, and cheerily exclaimed, "Good morning, sunshine!" to which I responded by letting him know he was number one, with my middle finger.

"Is that any way to greet your vacation partner?" Sneering at him again, I gave him a growl of distaste, and he pulled me into a hug. "I love you, darlin.'"

"If you truly loved me, you'd drive and let me sleep."

"Done." And for the three-and-a-half-hour drive, I snoozed to the faint sounds of eighties' hair bands playing in the background. A brush of skin against my cheek with my name spoken softly roused me from my sleep. "We're here, sweetheart."

Rubbing my eyes, I sat up and looked around. Surrounded by trees, we were atop a mountain with a small cabin in front of us. Gus stepped out of the car and opened the door for me. Extending his hand, he helped me out of the car. "It's beautiful here. I may not want to leave."

He shrugged. "If you want to move here, away from the world, I'm game." The idea of living in the mountains away from the rest of the world with Gus sounded appealing. Watching him pull the luggage out, I noticed how he'd trimmed down since rehab. He'd been working out a lot to keep himself from being home alone too much. I liked him with a little meat though. He gave the best hugs because he was soft and cuddly. When he caught me staring, he flexed his arm. "Are you checking out my new muscles?"

"Maybe. You look good, Gus-Gus. Then again, you always looked good." Blush crept up his cheeks and he smiled, a gleaming white perfect smile. His southern charm was the sexiest part about him. He deserved a good woman.

The inside of the cabin was decorated with black bears. From the curtains to the pillows on the couch, everything had a black bear on it. "I guess it's why they call this one Black Bear Hideaway."

"I brought some groceries, so we don't have to leave too much. Are you hungry? I can cook us some pancakes." A loud growl of hunger, as if on cue, roared from my stomach. "I brought chocolate chips and strawberry syrup for them."

"Mike's favorite?"

"The entire trip is about him, so I picked up his favorite foods." Unloading the groceries, I stocked the fridge with enough food for more than two days, at least as far as I was concerned. Gus was a hefty eater though. Everything Mike loved was there, including his favorite nonalcoholic beverage, Mountain Dew Code Red. Grabbing two bottles out of the pack, I poured them into cups of ice. "A toast to our friend. We miss you, buddy." Touching the two Solo cups together, we took a sip, our eyes fixed on each other.

After everything was unloaded, we went to relax on the couch. Gus sat on one end and I lay down with my head in his lap, my knees hanging over the other armrest. He peered down at me, running his fingers through my hair and I sighed. "It's peaceful here. Simple."

"Mike told me he stayed in a similar cabin with his wife. Black bears are apparently the big design detail here. I chose this one because it sounds like what he described. They came here because he won a trip on a radio station. It was the only way they could afford a honeymoon. They were so broke, they never left the cabin. He said it was the best trip ever."

"Did you know she was the only one he'd ever been with? Can you imagine never sleeping with more than one woman?" Gus cleared his throat avoiding my question. Sitting up, I touched his cheek turning his face toward me. "Have you only been with one woman?"

"I've never been with a woman, period. What my uncle did to me, it makes it hard to be intimate. I've never had the guts." I had an idea I should've probably thought over more before I acted on it though. Standing up, I straddled Gus's waist pressing my hands against his cheeks I leaned down capturing his lips with mine. His hands rested on my waist, pulling me against him as our mouths moved together. Nothing about the kiss felt sexual. When Gus's hand moved up and cupped my breast, we both broke out into a fit of laughter.

"I've never felt more awkward being kissed in my life," Gus said. "You're a beautiful woman, Angel. And I've wondered what it would be like to kiss you, but that was weird."

"Agreed. It would be so much easier if we enjoyed it. Why are we never attracted to the people who would make life simple?" Being in love with Gus would have made my life less complicated. Having gone through rehab together, we had a bond I'd never find with anyone else. Even though Marcus and I had made no promises to each other, kissing Gus left me feeling guilty inside.

"Wait. Were you just about to give me a sympathy lay?" Shrugging my shoulders, I smiled with a slight cringe hoping he wasn't mad at me. "You're so sweet. You know I thought grabbing your breast would make me hard, make it more real, but it was like copping a feel on my sister. Completely weirded me out."

"Me too. At least it's out of the way, we know where we stand." A small part of me was hurt by Gus's rejection. Mostly because it reminded me of Marcus stopping things between us and made me feel as though I'd lost my touch when it came to sex.

With his finger against my chin, Gus lifted my face to look up at him. "I know what you're thinking. I'm not rejecting your body. You're a great kisser and, darlin', you're sexy as hell. There's nothing wrong with you. What happened here is not what happened with Marcus."

I moved off his lap and took the seat next to him on the couch. "We don't know for sure. He sleeps with anything that breathes, and he won't sleep with me." He said he wanted to talk about what happened; hopefully, it was a good sign. Plus the fact he was jealous and questioning Cameron made me feel better too.

"You used to say that about yourself, and you wouldn't sleep with me just now."

Cocking my eyebrow at him, I replied, "Who straddled whose waist a moment ago?" Since the night with Marcus, I'd been wondering if romance was everything people painted it to be. When I slept around, I was unfulfilled and lonely, but I wasn't heartbroken and questioning my attractiveness. I wasn't sure which one was worse.

"You got a nap in the car, I think I'd like one now. Do you mind?" Gus yawned and stretched. "Give me two hours?"

"Sure. I brought a book to read. I'll curl up on the couch and relax. Have a nice nap, Gus-Gus." He leaned down and gave me a peck on the forehead before scooting off to the bedroom. Before leaving, I'd loaded up my Kindle with a few new reads in case I had trouble sleeping. In the book I started, I got through about five chapters before I set it down unable to connect with the story. Stepping out onto the back porch, I leaned against the railing staring out into the forest. A text came through just as I saw a deer walk into the field below.

Marcus: Having fun with your friend?

Me: Jealous? ;)

Marcus: Should I be?

Me: Well…

When he didn't respond, I had to ease his curiosity.

Me: No, Marcus. No reason to be jealous.

Marcus: Don't toy with me, Angel. I like you too much.

He liked me? I wasn't sure how to respond to his confession. I'd never had a guy say he liked me. I'd had them confess love, thinking it was the way to get in my pants, but never something as innocent and sweet as being liked. Tingles trailed across my skin. Never having known how it was to crush on a guy as a teenager, I was thrown back in time when I released a silly giggle. What was happening to me?

Marcus: Hello?

Me: I like you too, Marcus.

After typing my last message, I held my finger over the Send button for an eternity. In reality, probably only a minute, but it seemed like an hour. I stared at my phone, urging the bubble with the three dots to appear. They came only briefly before his response.

Marcus: Good. Now open the door so we can speak face-to-face.

Me: What the hell??

Quickly bolting through the back door, across the living room, to the front door, I slung it open to find nothing there. My phone dinged and I glanced down.

Marcus: See… not nice to tease, is it?

Me: Asshole.

As my heart tried to leap from my chest from anxiety, the smile on my face grew as wide as the Grinch making Christmas plans. A picture text came through with Marcus sticking his tongue out at me. I saved the photo and made it the background on my phone. The response I wanted to send would be a selfie of me looking angry, but I couldn't stop smiling long enough to take one.

"What put such a genuine smile on your face?" Gus asked, stepping out from the bedroom, stretching his arms above his head. Handing him my phone with the texts displayed, I watched his face as he read them. "So this is the famous Marcus? He's got a crazy long tongue." Jerking the phone out of his hand, I stared at the picture and noticed how right he was. "You're having pervy thoughts now, aren't you?"

"Me? Pervy? Never!" I winked at him and pulled him over to the couch. Resting my feet up on his lap as I leaned back, he lifted them and began to massage. "Remember how it freaked Mike out when you would massage my feet?"

"Yep. He thought it was too intimate an action and always asked if he should leave the room." We chuckled for a moment at the memory of Mike's thin face, large ears, and big goofy grin each time he teased us about being an old married couple who needed to get a room.

"You didn't nap long. Something on your mind?"

"The kiss before." Tensing up, I pulled my feet away from him and tucked them under my butt. "Don't worry. I'm not having feelings for you. I wanted to make sure we're the same after. Nothing's changed between us, right?"

"Right. Why would you think otherwise?"

"If it weren't for you, I'd be with Mike. I truly believe it. You've been my guardian angel, no pun intended. Our friendship is more important to me than anything else in this life." After leaving rehab, before Mike committed suicide, the three of us swore to always support each other. We promised no one would ever be alone again. Mike apologized in his letter for breaking his promise but asked us to stay together no matter what.

"You just try to get rid of me Gus-Gus and see how well you do."

"What about Marcus? If things get serious with you two."

"I can have friends. Any guy who won't let me have friends is not a guy I'm going to be with. So, to reiterate, you're stuck with me." No one could control me. My friends knew it was a fact, and Marcus would know soon enough if he tried. Gus grasped my wrist and pulled me forward to sit next to him. Turning my back to him, I lay against his chest as we sat reminiscing some more about our very short time with Mike.

TWENTY ONE

CAMERON

Most nights Marcus couldn't wipe the smile off his face. He was generally a happy guy. Since he found out Angel went out of town, he'd moped around the bar with a scowl. I caught him with a smile on his face for a moment as we were setting up for the evening.

"Nice to see you smiling again. Is there a reason?" I hoped he'd worked things out with Angel somehow.

"Been texting your girl a little. I'm anxious for her to come home so we can talk." Beer bottles clanked together as he loaded the cooler. I waited until the noise subsided before asking the tough question.

"And how will your talk go? You've never finished telling me what happened with your friend." Taking a glance at the clock on the wall, I checked to make sure we were ahead of schedule. "We don't open for an hour. Care to sit and talk?"

Marcus grabbed us two bottles of water and brought them to the table. Neither of us drank much anymore. Come to think of it, I hadn't seen Marcus drink in a while. I wondered if it had anything to do with his issue with Angel.

"Angel thinks I stopped the other night because of her, but it was all about me. I didn't have a condom, and it freaked me out."

"Safe sex is important. Why not just go out and get a condom? For future reference, I have a couple in my desk drawer." Marcus eyed me curiously. "Also, FYI, they glow in the dark, which is why I have them. My hubby and I don't use condoms anymore, but occasionally I surprise him in my office with a glowing dick waiting for him. I call it my own personal sex lightsaber."

Marcus burst out laughing, and I had to join in. "The complete definition of TMI right there. I needed the laugh though."

"So, tell me why the condom issue freaked you out so bad." Snorting with laughter, I clarified, "Your condom issue, not mine."

"Until a few months ago, I thought I was invincible. I never worried about things like diseases. Condoms were infallible as far as I was concerned."

"What happened a few months ago? Does this have to do with your friend Calvin's diagnosis?" We never talked about what stage

Calvin was in or how he coped with it.

"He's been on my mind a lot. We've known each other since we were three and he's always been my wingman. Lately, he's been living it up in New York City, different girl every week, sometimes two nights in a row. One thing we've never been is stupid. It's always 'wrap it before you tap it,' ya know?" Definitely a phrase I was familiar with. It dawned on me where this story might be headed, but I didn't interrupt his train of thought.

"He'd gotten lazy about it. Drinking too much and not thinking. Two times, out of probably a hundred, he knows he forgot the condom and did it anyway. Somewhere in that two percent of women, he contracted HIV."

The supreme asshole of STDs.

"The night he told me," Marcus continued, "was two nights after I slept with Bailey for the last time, and we hadn't used a condom because we were exclusive fuck buddies at the time. Scared the shit out of me, Cam. Two percent! He had a 2 percent shot of contracting something, and it happened. That's fucked up."

"Well, 2 percent isn't exactly… never mind, it's not important. I can see why you were freaked. But they're developing new drugs every day, and if your friend takes the meds like he should and keeps talking to the doctors, he may never develop full-blown AIDS."

"He tracked down the woman who gave it to him. Turns out, she knew she had it a week after they slept together and never tracked him down to get tested. She gave him Hepatitis C as well, and his HIV has already progressed significantly faster because of it. In the two years after he slept with her, there were literally a hundred women who needed to be tested, and he can't remember all of their names. He's a much bigger man-ho than I am, but it terrifies me to think of ending up that way."

In the short couple of years I'd known Marcus, I'd never seen him in such a panic. A stud with the ladies, confidence oozing from him, not a care in the world, that was the Marcus I knew.

"The other night, with Angel, I thought of Calvin, and I had to stop. Even though my first test was negative, it scared me to put her in that position. The first time we kissed, at Derrick's, I got carried away. I lost control, and if their baby hadn't interrupted us, we might've had sex right there. I slipped right back into my old ways. I've never cared about the girls I've been with before. It's been all about the sex. With Angel, I want her, but at the same time, I want to protect her. I'm sort of crazy about her, Cam. She's different from anyone I've met. As corny as it sounds I feel like there's a reason we met."

"Maybe I'm your fairy man-ho mother? Or something. After all, I'm the one who sent you to Tristan's house where you met her for the first time." Throwing him a wink, I watched as a blush crept over his cheeks. I'd never seen Marcus look embarrassed or act shy when talking about a woman before, it was rather adorable to witness.

"You should tell Angel what you've told me. I think… no, I know she'd understand. Is your friend Calvin getting the help he needs? Does he have the money for meds I mean?" Going untreated meant your lifeline was shortened tremendously.

"Barely. I want to help him, but I'm not in any position to help either. It costs him over a thousand dollars a month." I was angered by what was charged for the meds, which were so important, especially knowing how much of the cost was pure profit for the medical company.

Grabbing a leather pouch from my desk drawer, I unbound the tie and opened it up. Quickly scribbling with a pen, I wrote out a check for ten thousand dollars and handed it to Marcus.

"What is this?"

"My parents are loaded, let me share the wealth and do a good deed for a friend at the same time. If you want to go see him in New York, I'll book you a flight, my treat."

"Cam… I can't."

Hand in the air I stopped his argument. "You can. You will. First, tell Angel what is happening and tell her you want to see her when you get back from your trip. Leave tonight or tomorrow and be back in a couple of days."

"I can't leave without seeing Angel."

"She left without seeing you. Do what you need to do. She'll understand. Trust me." After Marcus agreed, he texted Angel about meeting her after his trip, and I booked him a flight leaving first thing in the morning.

Before leaving for the night, Marcus came into my office and gave me a hug. "Thanks again, for everything, Cam. I promise I'll repay you somehow for all of this." His lips twisted up and he squinted his eyes. "One more favor? Drive me to the airport in the morning?"

"I'm off the next couple of days, so yes I'll drive you to the airport."

TWENTY TWO

ANGEL

"If you still want to stay an extra day we can," I said to Gus after setting my phone back on the table. "Marcus is leaving town to see a friend in New York."

"We could check out early in the morning and go into Gatlinburg, do some touristy crap as you like to call it." Gus and I had spent the last several hours playing board games in front of a fire. Mike loved Monopoly and The Game of Life, and Gus had packed both. We'd exhausted ourselves running down memory lane and made the decision to take the scenic route home where we would spread Mike's ashes.

"Can we stay here for a few months? Maybe a year? Or forever even?" Two days with Gus had been stress free and simple. No anxiety, no worries, no pain from MS. Eventually I would miss my other friends, but I had to admit, at least to myself, how relaxed I was without having happy couples shoved in my face. Yes, I knew it sounded selfish. Their happiness was important to me, and I was so thankful they all found each other. But I was also jealous.

"You could stay here forever and never have sex?"

"They make BOBs for a reason." And I'd owned plenty of them, especially in the last year. Abstinence from any form of sex, even self-gratification, was too much to ask in my opinion.

"BOBs? Do I want to know?" As my friend Mary Jane would say, "Bless his heart." Gus was as pure a man as they come, and I loved that about him.

"Battery operated boyfriend." His eyes widened as pink filled his cheeks.

"Not to sound sappy, but don't you want more than robotic orgasms? From what you've told me, you've made a real connection with Marcus. Does it really matter how long it takes you two to have sex?" Gus had a valid point; the reality of it stung my pride a bit. Trying not to resort to assuming the woman's translation that he'd called me a slut, I took a deep breath and allowed his words to sink in.

"The sex is part of it, mostly because it's what I'm accustomed to. Being rejected isn't something I take easily. That being said, I do feel more than a sexual attraction to Marcus, and you're right, it could be enough. My friends, Gracie and Ashton, fell in love without sex being involved at first. I'm messed up, Gus. I don't know how to be with someone without offering myself to them." My voice caught in my throat with the confession. If I'd been sitting in front of a therapist, they'd call this admission a breakthrough. Gus had no words, only comfort as he wrapped me in his embrace. I clung to him, physically and emotionally as the words I'd spoken repeated in my head. *I'm messed up.*

Gus pressed his palms against my cheeks, focusing my attention on him. "I'm messed up too, sweetheart. If I wasn't, we wouldn't have met the way we did. I don't know about you, but I'm exhausted from today. We've run the gambit of emotions. Let's call it a night."

"I don't want to be alone right now."

"So don't be. Come cuddle with me." Taking my hand, Gus led me to the bedroom and tucked me in before slipping under the covers on his side of the bed. The king size bed left plenty of room for the both of us, but I wanted to be held. Sensing my need, or possibly seeing the puppy dog look on my face, Gus moved up behind me and slid his arm across my stomach, kissed my cheek and said, "Goodnight, Angel."

In the morning, I awoke to Gus still wrapped around me and snoring in my ear. It was a nice moment to open my eyes to a man I was familiar with, much like the morning I woke next to Tristan. His breath warmed my neck. I rolled over to face him and saw his mouth hanging open with a bit of spittle in the corner. "Gus-Gus." Softly whispering his name, I waited for his eyes to open. They widened, peered down between us, and sighed in relief. "Damn. What was that look?"

"I forgot we went to sleep together." Scrubbing his hands over his face, he covers his mouth with a yawn. "Ugh. I hope my dragon breath didn't choke you this morning."

"Oh please, I'm sure we could have a contest on whose is worse. Let's get up and head out to town. I'm ready to have a fun day with you."

Gus and I spent the day touring Gatlinburg, avoiding the moonshine tastings and the wineries. As evening hit, we took the scenic route home, sprinkling Mike's ashes in different spots in the mountains. I'd researched the laws on where it could be scattered legally, and in national parks, it was legal and common. For Gatlinburg, they only stated to choose undeveloped sections of the park to scatter the ashes.

On the way home, I offered to drive and let Gus sleep. He took me up on the offer without a moment of hesitation. The three plus hours trip home gave me a chance to think things over about Marcus. With him in New York, I had a few days to figure out exactly what I wanted to say to him.

"Wake up, sleepy head. We're here."

Gus woke up and looked around. "Where is here?"

"A Shot in the Dark. I need to talk to Cameron, and he's supposed to be waiting for me inside. Don't worry. I'm not going near the liquor.

Straight to Cam's office and he's going to drive me home." On the way back, I'd stopped for gas and sent a text to Cameron. He offered to meet me later on at home so I wouldn't have to step inside the club, but I told him I'd be fine.

I got out to give Gus a hug goodbye and I didn't want to let go. Three days locked away in a cabin with no outside interference had been exactly what I needed. With his arms around me, I squeezed tightly and whispered, "Thank you for the last few days. I had a wonderful time and needed the closure with Mike. Promise me we'll do better about having dinners together, not just when one of us wants to drink."

"I promise, darlin'." He kissed my forehead and caressed my cheek with his finger. "You take care of yourself. And good luck with Marcus." I watched him drive away and then scurried inside excited to see Cameron.

The moment I opened the door to his office I saw something I hadn't expected. "Marcus. What are you doing here? Aren't you supposed to be in New York?"

"My flight was postponed due to a snowstorm up north. But don't worry, I was just leaving." He moved passed me, and I grabbed his wrist. The sparks were still there as he stared at my hand on his. "I shouldn't be here, Angel."

"Why not?"

"I saw you with him. You don't owe me an explanation. We never made promises of monogamy or even agreed to a relationship. I only want to see you smile, and he puts a genuine smile on your face." My hand remained on his wrist; he hadn't tried to move away.

"Gus and I are friends *only*. But even if there was something between us, does that mean you wouldn't fight for me? Easy out for you to avoid all my baggage?" Attitude was something I resorted to when I felt rejection coming on. Walls raised, locks applied, I wouldn't let anyone touch me in my bubble.

Marcus grabbed the hand I waved around to accentuate my attitude and jerked me forward until our lips crashed together. His tongue snaked its way into my mouth, caressing mine. The strong embrace of his arms matched with the passion behind his kiss weakened my knees. Lost in the moment, Marcus had to bring me back to reality by gently pushing me away.

Caressing my cheek, he said, "I believe you're worth fighting for."

"We need to talk." *Why did those words always sound so detrimental?* Marcus had displayed such confidence, and the moment the words came out of my mouth, he deflated like a stuck balloon. "It's not bad, I hope." I wasn't sure how he'd respond to what I had to say. Feeling a need to put distance between us, I took several steps toward the desk, away from Marcus.

"If you don't even know if it's bad, then why should that instill confidence in me?" He smirked. I imagined it was due to leaving me speechless with his statement.

Why was this man so damn irresistible to me? I could love 'em and leave 'em as well as any stereotypical male player, but his presence left a mark I couldn't remove.

"There's something you should know about me before we try to do this romance thing, if that's even what you want to do after you hear what I have to say." I needed to be open about my life if I wanted anything real between us. Assuming he wanted the same thing as me seemed naïve considering he ran out just before we got down to the nitty gritty before.

Stepping toward me, in a pair of tight jeans I could only imagine he'd look even better from the back, I focused on his T-shirt about to burst open from the muscles begging to be shown off. The sexy smirk of confidence reappeared on his face as he took note of my ogling.

His soft fingers grazed down my cheek as he leaned forward placing a tender kiss on my lips. I was used to the rough make-out sessions from most men, including Marcus previously, but I found myself intrigued by the loving touch. "Rest assured, my Angel, I want you like I've never wanted any woman before. And I need to explain why I ran off the other night. It had nothing to do with you." His eyes looked up toward the ceiling in thought before he sighed. "Well, it wasn't entirely about you."

No words could've hurt more. He appeared to notice the pain in my eyes from his comment because he stroked my cheek. "Woman. You are the epitome of gorgeous. Everything about you screams sexy.

And your spitfire personality makes you even hotter. The reason it had to do with you is because I didn't want to hurt you."

"Let's stop dancing around this explanation and tell each other the truth before we make things worse." With a deep breath for courage, I said, "I have MS. Multiple—"

"Sclerosis, yes I know about MS," Marcus said finishing my sentence. "And I know you have it. I was worried about you after we decorated the bar, and he filled me in reluctantly on that one detail. It's one of the reasons I stopped the other night."

Ouch. Another stab to the ego. I knew he wouldn't want to be with me when he heard about all the baggage I'd be bringing. "And I expected it, which is why I wanted you to know. Don't feel bad, I—" And he instantly shut me the hell up with another electric kiss.

"Woman, I wouldn't care if you had leprosy, I'd still want you."

"I'm lost." And they said women were confusing.

"Sit down and stop tempting me with those lips." We sat together on the couch, our legs next to each other, his arm draped across the couch behind me. "My friend Calvin is HIV positive. Not only that, but he has Hepatitis C, which has developed into cirrhosis of the liver."

"I'm so sorry, Marcus." His admission took me by surprise. I expected something about not being strong enough to deal with everything going on in my life. I had to stop jumping to conclusions.

"The issue is it woke me up because he was a player like me, and I had to get my act together. I've been tested since I found out, and so far, it's come back negative. Since it's best to be tested more than once, three months apart, I go for a second test in a month."

"Have you been exposed?"

"Not that I'm aware of, but I've slept around, a lot."

"Preaching to the choir," I said with my hands in the air. "I'm no virgin, Marcus. I'm not proud of the numbers, but I have been tested and am also clean. I'm not sure I understand why you worry about me though?"

"You have MS, and you're a recovering alcoholic. The last thing I want to do is expose you to anything else. I didn't have a condom the other night. Even if I had, though, I'm not sure I would've gone through with it. We don't know each other well. I'm not professing my love for you, but I do care what happens to you, Angel."

"I care about you as well." He cupped the back of my neck bringing me in until our lips almost connected. At the moment, I wanted to rip his T-shirt in half and beg him to show no mercy in taking me right then and there. As much as I hated to admit it though, he was right. I didn't want to take the chance of being exposed to anything else.

"This can be a good thing, Angel."

"How?" I asked, our lips still close enough I could slip my tongue in his mouth if I wanted to. And I wanted to, but I held back.

"I want to know everything about the beautiful Hispanic woman who has starred in my fantasies for the past couple of months." Giving in, he took a taste of my mouth, and I fisted his T-shirt as my hands tried to push him away, though I seemed to be pulling him closer instead.

"We need a more public place. This office, where we almost screwed before, is bringing up too many memories." Marcus stood up and walked toward the door. Holding it open for me, he motioned me through. "Ladies first."

Extending his hand to me, I glanced down as though he were handing me an alien lifeform. "I thought I'd try the romance angle again. Hold hands. Too cheesy for you?"

"No. I just didn't expect it." Resting my hand in his, my fingers curled around his large palm, a sense of comfort washed over me. When it came to men, I'd always been on edge, ready to bolt at any moment to protect myself. With Marcus, I wanted to drop my protective barriers and let him be my shield from the rest of the world.

"I almost had a drink the other night, after you left. After more than a year of sobriety, I almost threw it all away. That terrifies me, Marcus. I'm telling you this because as much as it scared me, I still want to explore this thing between us."

My cards were on the table, all bets were off. He'd either give in to me or take everything I'd given and walk away. Marcus was quiet, but he still held my hand, so I hadn't lost faith yet. He led me through the back door of the club and out onto the sidewalk.

February in Nashville normally ranged from twenty- to thirty-degree highs during the day, but this year we'd hardly dipped below sixty. With the sun shining above and no breeze, it was a comfortable walk through the downtown area.

Due to the warmth of winter, the streets were filled with people enjoying their day. We continued walking with no destination planned, past the Ryman Auditorium, a venue known for its country music and other celebrities such as comedians. Reading the sign on the building, I noticed some of the names coming soon such as Carol Burnett, Norah Jones, and Ricky Skaggs. Marcus tugged me toward the edge of the sidewalk, and we waited for the light to change so we could cross the street. His silence weighed heavily on me.

"Where are we going?" I asked, unable to pretend to be interested in the local architecture we walked by, though I did love the Bat Building. A telephone slash cable provider owned the building, but the large beacons on top made it resemble Batman, which was how it gained notoriety.

"You wanted public, I'm starving, so I thought we'd have an early dinner at the Spaghetti Factory on Second Avenue. It's my treat. If you will, we can consider it a second date."

"Why were you being so quiet?"

"I wanted to surprise you." No one could blame me for ruining the surprise; we'd walked four blocks in silence. I needed to know he wasn't luring me to my death in the Cumberland River at the end of this road.

Being a Tuesday afternoon, the restaurant was fuller than I expected. Marcus put our names in and they said it would be an hour wait. Somehow, after flashing his smile with those beautiful dimples and a few words about how gorgeous someone's hair was, in French, we were seated within five minutes.

"You really do know how to get laid in every language. I thought you were kidding." Marcus winked and grabbed his napkin off the table tucking it into his shirt collar. I snorted with laughter at his makeshift bib.

"Nice look."

"You're the one who surprised me at work. I'm opening tonight so I won't have time to go home and change if I get sauce on me." The waiter took our orders. Since it was my first time here, I allowed Marcus to order for me.

One taste of spaghetti and I moaned as the melding of flavors coated my tongue. "I'm not sure taking things slow is in your vocabulary."

"Are you calling me a slut?" I asked, only half teasing.

"No, I'm calling you sexy as fuck. Don't do the woman-speak thing with me and twist my words. I have too many sisters for that shit." He pointed his fork at me as he spoke.

"Tonight I promise you're not getting more than a kiss on the cheek at the end of the date. We're going to challenge ourselves to have four dates before things get sexual. What do you say?"

Marcus raised his hand to his forehead, then moved it to mid-chest, and then to his left shoulder and lastly his right shoulder. "You're praying right now?" I asked with a chuckle.

"I need divine intervention to get me through the next three dates. You did mean four total making this the first, right?"

"Actually, we'll still consider this our second one." I had to giggle when his face lit up, knowing we had two dates down. "You know I went to Catholic school. I still have the uniform."

His eyes bulged as he made the sign of the cross for a second time and replied, "*Madre de Dios*," which meant Mother of God in Spanish. "I was agnostic before I met you, now I will do whatever it takes to have you in my life."

"If you make it to the fourth date, then we'll have a little dress up time." Lowering my voice, I leaned forward. "I owe you for the phone sex orgasm and the orgasm in the car, so you have a lot to look forward to. If I do say so myself."

"If we eat now and meet up in the morning for breakfast, would that be date three?" I chuckled at his eagerness. And then he added, "Cause I'm free for lunch tomorrow too," prompting me to guffaw, which drew attention from nearby customers.

The rest of the meal seemed to fly by with ease. We moved to safer conversation, unrelated to sex, for the remainder of our time together. Afterward, I walked Marcus back to the club in time for him to start his workday, and I called a cab and rode home with a smile on my face.

TWENTY THREE

CAMERON

With the next three days off, I made plans on what Addy and I would do to pass the time. I'd scheduled dates with Gracie and Autumn, a trip to the zoo, and an outing with Mary Jane, Craig, and Katelyn. We were social butterflies, painting the town, spreading fabulosity all over. Trust me; fabulosity was a word. The first day had been reserved for my favorite guy and girl.

Me: Addy and I want to have lunch with you.

Gavin: I'll be home in an hour. I love you

Me: I love you more.

I dressed Addy up in her Minnie Mouse dress, a black top with a red skirt filled with white polka dots, and black tights. Her Mary Jane shoes with a white bow set off the outfit perfectly. "You look beautiful, baby girl." She giggled in my ear as I lifted her onto my hip. "You ready to go have lunch with Daddy Gavin?"

"Yeah!" she cheered as I grabbed up her essentials bag. I refused to call it a diaper bag; young ladies don't wear diapers, and she was almost completely potty trained. I opened the door to step outside and Gavin stood in the doorway with a grin on his face. In one hand, he had a bouquet of roses, and in the other, he had a pizza. Looking us over he realized we had meant to go out.

"We can save this for tonight if you want."

"No, don't be silly. We'll eat it for lunch, and Addy and I will take a shopping trip to show off her new dress. The pizza smells delicious." Gavin handed me roses and leaned forward to steal a kiss before we sat down to eat. "Thank you for the flowers. What's the occasion? You always spoil me, but flowers are a rarity."

"No occasion. Lately, we haven't had much time together. Plus, I've been a bit of a downer and we've fought more than I ever want to do." With a gentle kiss against my cheek, he whispered, "I love you, Cam. You're my everything, and I'm sorry for how things have been lately."

"I love you too. You've been stressed, I understand completely. Now sit down and feed me pizza, I'm starving."

Addy munched away on her slice, painting her face with pizza sauce with each bite. Everything she did was adorable, and I could easily be entertained watching her. As I stared away, Gavin laid his hand on my shoulder. "Tell me how the matchmaking is going."

"The last I heard, not great. Angel went to the romantic getaway spot in our state with Gus, and Marcus hadn't told her what was freaking him out. She was supposed to be back in yesterday so I'm hoping they've worked things out. She texted me on the way home and asked me to meet her at the club. When I found out his flight had been canceled, I set it up for Marcus to be there in my place. I'm surprised I haven't heard from her, but I'm hoping that's good news." Throwing him a wink, he nodded.

"We all know your matchmaking can't be beat."

Gavin knew how much I butted in to be sure my girls ended up with their great loves. Our relationship's most important moments revolved around getting them their happily ever after. With Gracie, it was easy to manipulate the situations to bring her together with Ashton. For Mary Jane and Derrick, the distance made things a bit harder.

Mary Jane broke up with Derrick as soon as she decided she'd be leaving for Florida to take advantage of her Disney internship. After seeing how broken he was by her rejection, I asked Gavin to interfere. "Your brother looks like someone just killed his favorite puppy. He truly loves MJ, doesn't he?"

"He hasn't stopped talking about her since the day they met. There's no way he can up and move to Florida. If Katelyn wasn't a factor, he would in a minute though." Pressing my hands against his face, I focused his eyes on mine. "I have an idea." My part of the deal

was to talk to Mary Jane, which went nowhere because when the woman made up her mind, she was set in her decision. Gavin needed to have better luck with Derrick. Being that we were both great lovers of eighties' movies where the romantic gesture was key to the story, we had to convince him to go overboard in whatever way he could.

Gavin sent me a text requesting my presence at Derrick's house. The scene I walked in on was not what I expected. Shattered glass littered the living room floor. Luckily, Katelyn had stayed at Gracie's for the evening. Beer bottles were being smashed against the wall repeatedly causing the puddles of shards. "What the hell?"

Rushing over to me, Gavin fisted my shirt in a panic. "He's worse than I can handle."

"Derrick!" Next to a few shards of glass, I spotted drops of blood. I wrapped my arms around his middle, lifted him up, and shifted him toward the couch. "Your feet are cut up. You probably have glass stuck in them. Gavin, can you get a washcloth and first aid kit, please?"

A vacant expression filled his eyes, his face scrunched in sadness. My girl had demolished him, and she never knew it. "Talk to me, D. What is happening here?"

"Mary Jane's leaving, didn't you get the memo?" Slamming his head back against the couch, he cursed. "Fuck. The last four years, I've been fine with just Katelyn in my life. Where did MJ come from? Why did I let her get to me? She never felt for me what I'm feeling. Am I crazy, Cam?"

"Take it from me, she loves you. Before you argue, listen to me. MJ has never been in love. To hear her tell it, no one was ever interested. The truth is, she never could see her own beauty. She never noticed the men who wanted her. I saw her earlier tonight. I tried to convince her to talk to you. And you know what I saw?" Derrick shook his head. "Heartbreak. She loves you, and I guarantee she has no clue you feel the same. You need to show her."

"I can't ask her to stay, to give up her dream."

"Don't. You let her go. But before she goes, make sure she knows you love her. Let her know two years is nothing and there's still a chance for the two of you. She's stubborn, but worth the wait. When she makes her mind up about something, she sticks with it. And she puts everyone's happiness above her own. It's endearing, but frustrating at times as well. This time, she's put Katelyn's happiness first by telling you goodbye." Light returned to his eyes, hope filling his features again. "I'll text you as soon as I find out when she's leaving. You have at least a week to get something big together. A grand gesture she'll never forget."

The day Mary Jane left, I thought Derrick had chickened out until he showed up at the last moment with a personalized gift and a subtle, but obvious confession of love along with a sizzling kiss.

Mary Jane never knew I was the one who put the bug in Derrick's ear to wait for her. He had it so bad, so quickly, I think he would've waited for her whether I spoke to him or not, but I like to think I had a little something to do with her happiness. Two years later, I had my work cut out for me once again.

Pounding the door with my fists, I was getting impatient when there was no answer. "What the hell, Cam?" Derrick grunted as he flung the door open. I pushed my way inside and spun around on my heels to face him. "Come in, please," he said sarcastically.

"What's the grand gesture this time?" Clueless expressions were not attractive on Derrick. "For Mary Jane? You have to do the grand gesture thing again to get back on track. She's coming home."

"Before she left, we said we'd talk when she came back. I'm giving her space."

"Nope. Not going to work. Mary Jane says she wants space, but then, in her head, she contemplates everything that could go wrong and talks herself out of doing anything she's unsure of. After the funeral, she needs reassurance from you. I know her. She's panicked about seeing you again. It needs to be a surprise, or she'll talk her way out of it due to fear." I'd spoken to Mary Jane two nights ago, and she'd told me she didn't know what she wanted to do about Derrick. She loved him but was afraid he was ready to move on to someone new. Therefore I took matters into my own hands. I'd watched those two dance around love for two years, and it was time to jump all in.

"How can I surprise her?" For the next few minutes, we put together the plan for him to use the façade of Katelyn wanting to see her and using Ashton to deliver the message. The rest was history.

"Do you think Angel's story will end up as happy as Gracie and

Mary Jane's?" Gavin asked. He fed Addy a grape from a bowl he'd pulled out of the fridge sometime while I was reminiscing. "Or ours?" he grinned and gave me a wink.

"Pshh. No one will reach our level of happiness. We've bought cloud nine and aren't moving." If it were up to me, Angel would have the happiest ending of all of us. The tough part was, she had the biggest hand in getting there, and she'd been known to sabotage her own happiness out of absolute lack of confidence in herself.

TWENTY FOUR

ANGEL

Marcus kept his word after our third official date. He walked me to my door, leaned forward, and gave me the chastest, yet panty-dropping kiss on the cheek I'd ever experienced. After he dropped me off, I stepped inside, placed my back against the door, and slid to the floor with a grin on my face. One loud whoop from me, and Tristan was fumbling down the stairs in his boxers. He hit the bottom step before the turn in the stairs, put his hand on the rail, and jumped over the last three steps to get to me. "What happened? Did you fall?"

The panic on his face subsided the moment I glanced up smiling. "I'm better than I've been in a very long time. And damn, that was impressive just now." We bumped fists, and he occupied the floor next to me.

"What, or who, has put that smile on your face? I'd like to thank them. It's been a long time since I saw such a beautiful sight." He pulled me into his arms, my head on his shoulder, and gave me a squeeze. "Seriously, what's happened?"

"Marcus. We had our third date today. This could be it for me, T. I might finally get my happy ending. I know it's probably too soon, but—"

"Who says it's too soon? Looking back, I knew I was in love with Lanie after the first night we spoke. Mary Jane has said the same thing about Derrick. She knew the day they met at the park. Marcus is a good guy." Lanie appeared at the top of the stairs wearing a robe she had just finished tying shut as she descended. "Shit. Sorry, babe, Angel's fine."

"So I see. Since we're all together, I thought we could talk about the house situation." From the lack of real clothes between the two of them, it was clear I'd interrupted their late night quickie or sexcapades, whatever the case. Living in the same house wasn't fair to the married couple. I feared I couldn't afford to live on my own though. "Angel?"

"Lanie and I found two houses we absolutely love, and we wanted to show them to you." I opened my mouth to reject the idea, but Tristan stopped me. "Look at them first, then decide."

I allowed Tristan to help me up and followed them into the living room to pull up the houses on the computer. Seven tabs were open.

"Sorry, I was researching things earlier." Before she closed one of the tabs, I noticed the page heading. Tristan didn't seem to see it so I decided to ask Lanie about it later in case he was unaware.

"This one's our favorite. It has a garage in the back with a full apartment above. It's slightly higher than we can afford, but if we charge you the rent you pay now, we can get by. Tristan still has a little inheritance for a down payment. If you don't want to come with us, we have a backup plan. But Angel," Lanie turned and grasped my hands in hers, "Please consider it."

Music blared from Tristan's pocket. "It's my dad. I'll take this in the other room." His relationship with his father had come so far since his mother passed. Instead of groaning when he saw his name on caller ID, most days it made him almost grin. He was helping Macy pay for college, which took a load off Tristan financially too.

"The page you closed before. Does Tristan know you're researching that topic?" She sucked her lips between her teeth and held back tears as her head shook. "Should I be worried?"

Swallowing hard, Lanie choked back a sob. "After Tristan's mom passed, I talked to his dad about signs the Alzheimer's had started to affect her. I've been pressing Tristan to get tested for the markers, but he says he doesn't want to know. He's afraid knowing will make him different."

"Why do you want to know? I kind of understand his reasoning. Why would you want to question everything he does? When he forgets where he left his car keys, you're going to think it's a sign. If he stumbles over the name of something simple, you'll start counting the days you have left." I whispered to keep Tristan from hearing me.

"He wants to start trying to have children, Angel." She paused to listen for Tristan. His voice could be heard chatting away in the other room. "I'm terrified of giving my children a life of doubting their father's love because of a disease."

"So instead you'd rather never have children and worry every day about when Tristan will forget you exist?" I placed my hand on hers and said, "You and Tristan need to decide this together because, in the end, it will affect you both. But, this shouldn't stop you from having children, no matter what the outcome."

"I promise I'll talk to him about it again." We heard Tristan saying goodbye from the other room, and Lanie stopped whatever she was about to say, and I changed the subject back to the house hunt.

"Are you two sure you want me to live with you? What happens if I move out?"

"We'll deal with it. The truth is, we can afford the payment without your help, but we know you wouldn't accept living with us free, so we thought the same payment would work out." Even if I never found my prince charming, I was the luckiest girl in the world because I had the best friends anyone could ever want.

"What did I miss?" Tristan asked as he returned to the room. "Did you talk her into it, Lanie?"

"She did," I replied confidently. "Schedule a time we can go check it out. You know my work hours. I'm going to hit the sack. It's been a long day, and I'm a little sore." While Tristan called their real estate agent, Sam, I leaned down and said, "You'll be fine. No matter what happens, you have a great support system." I kissed her cheek and hugged her quickly before heading upstairs.

A year ago, no one could have convinced me Lanie and I would be so close. The little things she did for me meant more than anything. She painted my toenails for me with the façade it was a girl bonding moment between us, but I knew it was because she'd seen how much I struggled with muscle pain after painting them during one of my relapses. Whenever it came time for groceries, she would insist on taking care of the bill swearing she owed me money for something, but I knew it was because she'd heard me talking about the medical bills I was still paying off. And when my medicine ran low, she would pick up my new prescription before I even realized it was time. Lanie may have come into the group only recently, but she was easily one of my best girlfriends, as close as Mary Jane and Gracie were to me.

TWENTY FIVE

CAMERON

ainy days were lazy days for me. Since I had the day off, I was content to stay inside and curl up on the couch watching movies all day. Gavin came over to kiss me goodbye before he left for a meeting. "What are you going to watch this morning?"

"I think it's time to introduce Addy to John Bender."

One eyebrow raised, Gavin stated, "She's three. I think *The Breakfast Club* is a little beyond her comprehension level." Lowering my eyes, I pushed my bottom lip out and gave my best sad-puppy face. "I didn't say you couldn't watch it, but maybe have *Moana* playing on the iPad." My husband was a genius at multitasking, in all forms of life.

With our daughter grossly entertained by the blocks on the floor, I pulled Gavin to the side. Pressing him against the hallway closet, I whispered, "Mary Jane offered to take Addy for the night so when you come home tonight be ready to make up for lost time." It had been weeks since we'd had sex. Between the bar, Gavin traveling for work, Addy, and me trying to hook up Angel with Marcus, we hadn't had a moment to ourselves.

Peering around the corner, Gavin checked on Addison once more before our lips crashed together in a frantic dance. We didn't mind simple kissing in front of Addy, but sometimes we wanted a private moment to enjoy each other fully. Gavin's hands moved toward the hem of my shirt and slipped inside. His fingers trailed across my skin sending tingles up my spine. "You need to get to work before we get out of hand. Plus, little bit is here."

He kissed me on the nose and said, "To be continued. I love you."

Quietly rounding the corner, he snuck up on Addy and picked her up in a fit of giggles as he flipped her over and planted kisses on her cheek. "I love you, little bit. Daddy will see you tonight."

After Gavin left, I picked up the phone to call Mary Jane. "Are you still able to take Addy tonight?"

"Absolutely. Katelyn's looking forward to it. Derrick is going to pay her to babysit. Don't worry. We'll be there the entire time. She wants to be a grown-up babysitter so we're letting her give it a shot."

Katelyn was eight years old and loved Addy like a sister. Once at a restaurant she even called Addy her sister when the waiter asked. It never bothered me. Mary Jane never tried to take Addy from us or stake a claim to her. None of us were sure if Katelyn understood what Mary Jane had done, or how technically Addy was Craig's sister by blood. One day, when they were all older, we'd explain the story.

In the beginning, Mary Jane was a bit timid about coming around Addy for fear of growing too attached. But she had distanced herself enough in the pregnancy to understand the baby wasn't hers and eventually formed a special bond with her goddaughter. Her resemblance to Mary Jane was uncanny. It would have been hard to deny their connection once Addy was old enough to see it too.

"Sounds great. I'll see you tonight, then." Still playing with the set of blocks, I watched Addy for a moment before stepping out to grab a movie. *The Breakfast Club* always set on the top shelf of my bookcase because I watched it at least monthly, sometimes weekly. Following Gavin's advice, I put *Moana* on the iPad for Addy, and I curled up in the chair to watch my movie.

Drifting off to sleep with visions of John Bender dancing in my head, I was awakened by a knock on the door. Briefly, I checked on Addy; she'd curled up on the floor next to me with her thumb in her mouth and fallen asleep. The sweet sucking sound made me smile. Standing in the doorway was no one I expected to see. "Marcus? What's up?"

"Hey, boss man. Can I come in?" I shushed him and dragged him in the door. "Sorry," he whispered. Spotting Addy on the floor, he pointed at her and gestured lifting her up. I nodded for him to go ahead. Cradling her in his arms, he carried her back to her bedroom and laid her down, then shut the door. "Glad I didn't wake the little princess."

"Me too. She's has a playdate tonight. What brings you by?" He followed me into the kitchen, and I grabbed a soda for both of us. Hopping up on the counter, he crossed his legs in front to steady himself. I joined him on the opposite countertop. "Women troubles?"

"Just the one. We've been on three dates now, and I can't figure out what to do for the fourth. It needs to be romantic. It's the big number we said we'd make it to before sex. We've been taking it slow so far. The other night I kissed her cheek goodnight."

"Damn, why run when you can crawl through life? But I get it, and I approve. I know about the first date. How did the second and third go?" Marcus filled me in on the date at the Spaghetti Factory. For the third date, they'd gone to a movie and dinner at a local diner. Knowing Angel the way I did, I knew the lack of intimacy was getting to her, but she wanted slow and romantic, so she'd have to be patient.

"I could sit here and give you a breakdown of all her favorite things, but you should be yourself." I'd played matchmaker before, but there's only so far my skills could take a relationship. The two people involved had to make it work if they wanted it to last. I might have given my friends a push or two, but eventually, they'd have ended up together anyway. Fate was something I fully believed in.

"Do you know if she's busy tonight? We've been spacing our dates to at least a week apart trying to take it slow. It's been a few days since our last one, but I'm anxious to see her again. I wanted to surprise her by dropping by unannounced with maybe dinner and roses?" Holding up my finger toward him, he nodded understanding. I sent Angel a text.

Me: Angel girl, what are you up to tonight?"

Angel: Nothing. Staying in my pajamas and watching movies I guess.

Me: Sounds exciting….

Angel: Bite me. Do you need a sitter?

Me: MJ is taking Addy for the night. I'm having sex with my hubby later.

Angel: Sounds much better than the night I have planned.

"She's free as a bird tonight. You should go to the store, get fresh ingredients, and show up ready to cook dinner for her. Something you can mix up together and then let it cook in the oven for a while giving you time to talk or cuddle on the couch. Maybe lasagna or chicken and veggies? Can you cook?" Spouting off suggestions, I noticed Marcus's eyes glazed over either taking mental notes or wondering how he could pull this off.

"Yep, a few things at least. Being raised Italian I should be able to pull off the lasagna, and garlic bread will keep us from making out too much." I snorted at his logic. The first meal Gavin and I had was filled with garlic and onions, and we barely kept our hands off each other. "I gotta go. Wish me luck!" And in a flash, Marcus was out the door on his way to prepare for his big move.

Thirty minutes after Marcus left, I was seated watching the rest of my movie when my phone rang. "Angel throw you out already?"

"No, man. I'm at the store looking at flowers. Do I go for the cliché red roses?" Amateur. Red roses were romantic, but not inventive.

"Do they have any Gerbera daisies?" From the silence on the other end of the line, I knew I needed to rephrase my question. "Do they have any colorful petal flowers in a bunch?"

"Yep. They look like daisies but are blue and pink and green?" They were the same flowers Gavin bought me the night he proposed.

"Bingo. Grab those and grab a bottle of sparkling cider."

"Won't she be offended at the sight of a fake wine?" Some might, but Angel would consider the gesture thoughtful.

"Nope. And if she does, tell her it was my idea." The doorbell rang as soon as I hung up with Marcus. "Geez. I'm too popular today." The unexpected visitor picked the wrong moment to show up. "Angel, I thought you were staying in to relax this evening?"

"MJ called. She forgot they had a meeting at Katelyn's school and asked if I could take Addy for a bit, and they would pick her up. She wanted to make sure you and Gavin had your romantic night." Spinning around I dragged her to the bedroom and snatched up

Addy who'd been sitting up playing with a stuffed animal in her bed. "Daddy Cam!" she called out.

"Angel is going to play with you for a while so Daddy Cam and Daddy Gav can have a playdate. Won't that be fun?" Addy cheered and raised her hands up for Angel to lift her. I shuffled around grabbing up her necessities and tossing them in a bag. Next, I shoved Angel toward the front door. "Have fun, sweet girl!" I kissed Addy and started to close the door behind Angel.

"Dang, Cameron, I guess it's been a while. Get it, girl!" she chuckled, and I gave her a thumbs up and closed the door. Hopefully she'd make it home before Marcus showed up. At least with Addy around, they'd stick to taking it slow. They wouldn't get it on while my child was in the house. "Shit." I opened the door and screamed for Angel, but it was too late. She was pulling out of the driveway. "They better not have sex around my baby girl," I stated to an empty room.

After sending a quick text to Marcus to warn him of Angel's evening plans changing, I jumped in the shower to get ready for the night with my man. Lost in my musical stylings bouncing off the walls I didn't hear the door open. I turned around to rinse my hair. When my eyes opened, Gavin stood in the shower with a smile on his face. Stepping forward his fingers skimmed my cheek before he leaned in and captured my lips with his. We were in for quite a night.

TWENTY SIX

ANGEL

On the way to the house, I stopped and picked up a happy meal for Addy and a large milkshake for myself. Nights on the couch had become the norm for me over the last year. I didn't mind having the time to myself, but I was glad to have Addy's company. Tristan was working at the bar and Lanie was doing teacher conferences at her school, so it would be just the two of us in the house.

A few minutes after we arrived home, Marcus showed up. "Hi. I brought dinner if you aren't busy." He smiled.

"Angel!" I was beckoned from the other room by a tiny voice.

"Oh, you have company?"

"Addy's here for a couple of hours. Please come in. If I'd known you were coming by, I'd have fixed myself up a little." Not worrying about my appearance, I'd driven to Cameron's wearing yoga pants and a men's white tank top.

"You look beautiful. Have you eaten?" In his hands were plastic grocery bags full of vegetables and noodles and several other things I couldn't see clearly. "I'm here to make you my famous lasagna."

Impressed by the gesture, I took a bag from him and led him to the kitchen. After setting it down, I went to grab Addy from the living room. "Say hi to Uncle Marcus."

Marcus stepped forward and flirted with Addy, giving her his killer smile and telling her how adorable she was. If she wasn't a toddler, I'd be a little jealous of the attention he gave her. Addy grinned and blushed when Marcus kissed her little chubby hand. Leaning forward, she wanted to be in Marcus's arms. "Traitor," I mumbled as he scooped her up.

Marcus winked at me. "Kid, can you help me make lasagna?" She nodded, and he kept her on his hip as he unloaded the bags one-handed and threw requests out for the dishes he needed me to supply. As Marcus worked and held Addy, he sang a song to her in a language I believed was Italian.

"That's not a dirty song you're singing, is it?" I teased, referring to his comment about knowing how to get laid in any language.

He chuckled and shook his head. "What kind of weirdo would I be to sing a dirty song in front of a three-year-old?" He kissed Addy's cheek. "It's a song my mom used to sing to me."

Pressing my back against the wall, I watched the scene in front of me. Addy's head was on his shoulder, her little chubby arm wrapped around his neck. She was enchanted by Marcus, and I couldn't blame her. No one else had ever had a role in the future I saw for myself. Marriage, family, they were never in the cards. I'd imagined I would continue my life of one-night stands until no one wanted me and I'd die alone. A depressing thought, but one I'd had many times.

In the moment, I envisioned Marcus holding onto a different child. One with olive-colored skin, dark hair, a child with features matching us both equally. Had I fallen harder for him than I realized? Lost in fantasy, I was pulled out by the doorbell. "I'll get it." I raced to the door, running away from the dream in my head.

"Hey, MJ. Come on in. Addy's in the kitchen helping Marcus cook."

Mary Jane stepped past me in the doorway and pulled me aside to the living room. "Before we go in there, I want the scoop. Are things going well with you and Marcus?"

I was unable to hide the happy grin on my face, and Mary Jane bounced up and down with excitement, silently so Marcus wouldn't hear. "I can't express how happy I am about you two." She wasn't the only one. For the first time, possibly in my entire life, I had hope for my future. It wasn't something to be frightened of.

Marcus came around the corner and whispered, "Hey, MJ." Addy was asleep in his arms. "She just fell asleep. I think I bored her with my singing."

"I think you hypnotized her with it. You had me in a daze," I admitted with a grin.

Mary Jane watched the exchange of smiles between Marcus and me and then stepped forward to take Addy. "You guys enjoy your evening. I'll take over babysitting and will make sure to let Cameron and Gavin know what an amazing job you two did." She quickly grabbed the diaper bag and shuffled out the door. "Good night," she whispered and then closed the door.

"Wow, she took off quickly," Marcus remarked. "Was it something I said?"

Stepping forward, I placed my hand behind his neck and brushed my lips against his. He pulled me closer, intensifying the kiss. When we came up for air, I gazed into his eyes and said, "No one will be home for hours. I'm tired of taking it slow."

"I still have a week before—"

"Before your second test, I know. Your first test was negative, and you took it months after the last time you had intercourse. The chances of your second test being positive are slim to none." He still seemed unsure. What he didn't know was I couldn't sleep the other night and used the time to research HIV testing to find out as much as possible. All the research said the disease could take a few weeks to show up in your system. Marcus said he hadn't been intimate for six months before he ever took the first one. Fear was dictating our relationship, and I wanted to put a stop to it.

"We're going to use condoms. I want this, Marcus. Most people are only tested after being told they were exposed. You don't know that you've ever been exposed. It's a precaution, and it's a good one to take, but I wouldn't put myself in danger of gaining another lifelong illness if I didn't feel the chances were slim to none. Even slim is pushing it." And to seal the deal, I pressed my lips against his once more.

"I was waiting for the oven to preheat before I put dinner in. Give me two seconds to put the lasagna in the fridge and turn off the stove. We can cook it later." Marcus disappeared, and I heard the fridge door open and close before he reappeared a moment later.

"Lead the way," Marcus replied. I took his hand and guided him up the stairs to my bedroom. We stood by the bed not saying anything, just looking at each other like two nervous teenagers about to lose their virginity. I went to remove my shirt, and Marcus stopped me. Sweeping my hair off my shoulder, he bent to kiss the nape of my neck, following a trail across the exposed skin. My hands moved to unbutton his shirt. I slipped my hands inside to feel the ridged muscle beneath.

Gazing into my eyes, Marcus whispered, "I've never felt this way about anyone in my life, Angel. Those words people say in this moment, the three simple words that make up the most powerful phrase in the world, I want to say them right now. I'm so scared it's too soon, so just know I'm feeling it, but not ready to say it out loud."

With his thumb, he swiped away the tear on my cheek. If there was such a thing as a soul mate, I knew he was mine because I felt the same exact way. I raised my arms above my head, and he took the hint to remove my shirt. No more words were spoken between us. Our bodies spoke for us. Pulling me against him, his mouth continued the trail across my shoulder, removing my bra strap, letting it drop off. Gliding his hands up my back, he unhooked my bra with one flick of his hand. When he threw me a confident wink, I laughed, and his lips met mine as though he were trying to taste the laughter.

My breasts fell free of the lace holding them, and Marcus moved his mouth down to capture one nipple while his thumb and index finger worked on the other. Tugging my fingers through his hair, I pulled him harder against me, wanting more. His hand moved from my nipple and trailed down my body until he cupped the warmth between my legs. My legs grew weak as he massaged me over the thin material of my yoga pants. I pushed away from him, taking a seat on the bed beside us. Grabbing his belt buckle, I pulled him forward. Unbuckling his belt, I rolled my eyes up to watch him as I unzipped his jeans and freed him from the confines. I expected to find sexy boxer briefs, but he'd gone commando. I wondered if it was just for me or a normal occurrence. Either way, it was hot knowing there'd been so little material between us. I reached for the drawer of my nightstand and pulled out a box of condoms. Marcus bit back a gasp as I rolled the condom over his length. Taking the tip of him in my mouth, I heard him suck in a breath and watched his eyes roll back in pleasure as I moved inch by inch until I had swallowed him fully.

When I felt him begin to tighten, ready to spill, I stopped. He pushed me back on the bed and quickly removed my pants. Leaving me on the bed in nothing but my panties, he pushed apart my knees and moved between them. Peppering kisses along my thigh, I pressed upward wanting his mouth on my core. A moment later, I felt his tongue graze the edge of my panties as he traced the lines, and then his finger dipped beneath the thin material. Just as his finger pressed inside me, I felt his tongue touch my clit and I bucked upward. Within seconds, I was orgasming with my hand pressing against the back of his head as he continued moving his tongue in magical ways, soaring me to heights I'd never reached.

He made a move I wasn't expecting. Placing his hands on my hips, he rolled me over to the side and bent down to kiss my left cheek. "You do have a mole right in the center." I loved that he remembered such a trivial detail of one of the first conversations we had.

"I can't believe you remember me saying that."

"I remember everything about you," he whispered just before nipping at my skin and flipping me back over.

My panties flew across the room, and Marcus climbed above me. He kissed me and I tasted myself on his tongue. In a swift movement, he was inside me. I shrieked at the sharp pain it caused. It had been a while since I'd had sex, and Marcus was not a small man. Pausing a moment, he looked to me for reassurance, and I said, "Don't stop now."

Sex was nothing new to me. I'd had more partners than I cared to admit. But in that moment with Marcus, I knew what people meant about the difference between having sex and making love. As cheesy as making love sounds, it's more erotic than sex ever could be. The depths of emotions crashing with the raw passion and intensity of our bodies as they connected made the orgasm more than just a momentary blissful feeling, and more like I was floating in a different world surrounded by nothing but happiness. I knew what I'd been missing by having sex without love.

After removing the condom, Marcus collapsed beside me, pulling me into his arms and throwing a blanket over us. Wrapping my arm across his chest, I placed my head against his shoulder. "I feel it too, but I'm not ready to say it either." Grinning at me, he kissed my forehead and together we drifted off to sleep.

TWENTY SEVEN

CAMERON

With sunlight peeking through the curtains, I rolled over to see if my love was awake. Gavin was on his back with his arms bent at the elbows resting behind his head. His washboard abs were uncovered, the sheet barely resting over his lower half, leaving a view of his sexy V. He looked like a model from a magazine. I traced my fingers over his chest, loving the feel of his skin. A grin filled his face letting me know he'd woken up. "That feels nice."

"*You* feel nice," I said before leaning over and planting a kiss on his beautiful lips. "We haven't had a night so wild in a long time. As much as I enjoyed it, I miss our girl."

Gavin pulled me against him, and I wrapped my arms around

his body. "I miss her too. But I love having this time with you. We've lost a lot of time together this year. Between the club, my work, and dealing with homophobic assholes, I feel I've neglected you."

"We've neglected each other. It hasn't just been you. I've been spending a lot of time with my friends instead of my husband lately." Propping up on my elbow, I traced lines across his chest as I talk. "Things need to change. I want to dedicate at least two nights a week for the three of us. Just you, me, and Addy. Doesn't have to be anything drastic, just eating dinner together and watching movies. Phones off, no interruptions."

Gavin brushed his lips against mine and replied, "Sounds perfect." He rolled over, grabbed his phone, and unlocked the screen. "I'm taking it one step further." His fingers flittered across the screen. With his tongue sticking out of the corner of his mouth, his eyebrows furrowed, he typed away without explanation. Instead of being my usual nosey self, begging for details, I took a moment to appreciate his adorableness. In my life, I'd used humor and flamboyancy to cover my pain. Since I met Gavin, I didn't need to hide anymore. I could be me. I loved who I was with him. He brought out the best in me and loved my craziness. Even with the homophobes we dealt with too often, he never asked me to tone down my personality or change anything about myself. I loved him more than I imagined I could.

Turning the phone toward me, he showed me what he'd been doing. "New York?" Gavin nodded. "You want to take a trip?"

"I want to go back to where we shared one of the best days. The place we married. And I want to share it with Addy. She may be too young to understand, but I think we need this." His idea sparked one within me. He had awoken my inner matchmaker. "What's going on in that beautiful head of yours?" he asked. He knew me too well.

"Marcus had to postpone his trip to New York due to snow. He hasn't rescheduled yet. What if we ask Angel to come along too? Marcus could visit his friend, and Angel could give us a little time alone while we're there by taking care of Addy. We'll treat for everyone." I paused a moment before I added, "I'm sorry, you probably want this to be family only."

"Don't be silly," Gavin began, "Angel is family. And so is Marcus truthfully. I think it's a fantastic idea. Now you get to be in charge of convincing them to go." He kissed me and grinned. He knew how stubborn Angel could be.

We wanted to make plans as soon as possible, so I got dressed and went straight over to speak to Angel while Gavin went to the Collinses to pick up Addy. When I arrived, it took a moment for someone to answer the door. Lanie opened in with a smile. "Hey, Cam, what brings you here this morning?" She pulled me inside and shut the door.

"I was looking for Angel. I wanted to talk to her about something.

Is she here?"

"I think she's still asleep. She was in bed when I got home last night, and her door hasn't opened since. I didn't want to bother her in case she's having an MS spell." We all knew how sporadic the pain was and tried to be as accommodating as possible without smothering or ignoring her. "I'm off this morning, if you'd like to have a cup of coffee with me, I'd love the company."

"If you have some of that chocolate cherry blend, I'd love a cup."

"Tristan just bought a new box at the store a few days ago." Lanie linked her arm in mine and led me to the kitchen. She made us each a cup of coffee. The room smelled of chocolate and cherries as the first cup brewed. She handed me a steaming mug and sat next to me. "Do you remember the first time we met?"

"You and Tristan were having an afterhours date at the club. You freaked out a bit worrying he would get in trouble."

She laughed. "True, I did. I guess I should have asked if you remembered our first talk. When you came to bring me the tape from Tristan."

Lanie had overheard an angry tirade from Angel where she admitted she'd slept with Tristan. They weren't together when it happened, they hadn't even met, but he'd fibbed about there being any romantic history with Angel. In his defense, it was a drunken night of sex, no romance involved. Tristan had asked for my help, and together we'd made a mixtape for her. He asked me to deliver the note and tape with a player but to leave without bothering her. He didn't want to crowd her.

I'd never been the best at following instructions. I'd always gone my own way just as Fleetwood Mac told me to. When I arrived at Lanie's, I rang the doorbell. Her hair was a mess and her eyes barely slits as they were swollen from crying. "Lanie, do you remember me?" I asked when she opened the door.

Pulling her robe closed, she reached up with her free hand and swiped the hair out of her eyes. "You're one of Tristan's bosses, or his friend maybe?"

"Technically both. Right now, I'm here as a friend. He asked me to deliver this to you." I held out the clear cassette tape box with the letter underneath it. When her forehead scrunched in confusion over the tape, she started to speak, but I held up the player. "I can time travel, in case you didn't know that about me." I winked.

"Thanks for this, but—"

"One thing about me is I'm a fantastic friend, but a terrible listener. So, could I come in and talk to you for a minute?" After a moment of silence—I assumed she was thinking it over—she stepped aside and waved me in.

"Would you like some coffee?" Lanie asked. Her voice sounded a bit scratchy. I'd seen this heartbroken look on all my girls at some point. At the time, I had no idea if Lanie and Tristan would reconcile.

"I'd love some. My name is Cameron, by the way." The wonderful *smell of chocolate and cherries filled my nose for the first time on that day. "That smells amazing."*

"I found it at a little shop in Gatlinburg. They had it out for sampling. Normally I hate black coffee, but this one needs nothing added to it." From the first taste, I knew she was right. "Look, Cameron, you're very sweet to deliver this letter for Tristan, but I don't know what you could say that he didn't try to say earlier."

"What I can't tell you is how you feel or what you should do. But I'm going to tell you about my friend Tristan. For the past five years, he's been raising his baby sister while his mom's memory fades and after his father abandoned him. He's been through more than most anyone should go through before their twenties. Because of all that, when he moved here and gained us as a family, he was able to let loose a little and make up for the youth he missed out on. He's been sleeping around since he arrived in town." I saw the way she twitched uncomfortably. "That was before he met you. Since the day you came into his life, we haven't been able to get him to shut up about the 'auburn-haired beauty' he met at the bar. As much as we moaned and groaned though, we've all been happy to see him getting back to his old self. You brought him back. You grounded him. And we're grateful to you for it."

"He lied to me, Cameron. I don't like liars."

"He didn't technically lie. And yes, I know it's not comforting to hear excuses, but his night with Angel was in no way romantic or memorable. Neither of them remembers it at all. He's not proud of

the night, mostly because he feels he took advantage of a dear friend. I haven't known Tristan for long, he's relatively new to our little family, but he's one of the most caring guys I know. Do you know the story about my daughter, Addy?"

She shook her head. "Mary Jane was a surrogate for our daughter. She carried her while working in Florida and Tristan was by her side every day. He fell in love with her, but never said anything because she was in love with Derrick. Even though he knew nothing would ever happen between them, he was her rock. He was instrumental in getting Derrick and MJ back together."

"He told me he feels their closeness confused his feelings. He'd never had such a loyal friend before, and he mistook it with being in love. Can I still believe that considering his lies?" Lanie posed a logical question, but only Tristan could answer to his true feelings.

"If those were words from his mouth, I'd consider them true. He's not a liar, Lanie. He's simply a man with regrets. I think you can understand the feeling." Mary Jane had confided in me about what happened with Lanie at the funeral of Derrick's father. Lanie and Derrick had been on a couple dates, but it didn't work out. At the funeral, Lanie met Mary Jane and tried to imply the relationship was more than simple dates. She acted catty and rude in an effort to hurt Mary Jane and cause a rift in her relationship with Derrick. I could see the embarrassment streak across Lanie's features and knew she understood what I meant. "Do me a favor. Listen to this tape and go to Tristan."

"I don't need to listen to it. He wrote the songs on the back, and I know all the lyrics so I get the message. How do I return the gesture?"

"I'm glad you asked!" Eighties movies were my life, and I would get these two back together with the help of my favorite eighties' figure, John Bender. Lanie got dressed in pink, and after a quick run to the store, she headed toward his house with a magnetic diamond earring in her hand.

"You're quite the matchmaker, Cam. Tristan and I might not be together if it weren't for your interference back then." Though I enjoyed taking credit for my matchmaking skills, I knew they'd have ended up together no matter what I said. Fate was a powerful puppet master.

"Something on your mind? I saw a bit of concern in your eyes."

"I've been doing a lot of research on Alzheimer's lately. And I've been trying to figure out a way to talk to Tristan about getting tested. No one else knows but Angel. You give the best advice though, tell me what you think."

"I think we spend too much time worrying about the future and not enough living in the now. Say the results come back positive, what will it change?"

Lanie shrugged and shook her head. "Is *not knowing* any better though?"

"If he tests positive for the gene, it's not going to tell you when it will happen. Do you want to live in fear of each day wondering if he still remembers you? Or would you rather live each day enjoying your time together? Taking the test won't change his diagnosis, but it could drastically affect your future."

"How do you always know the right things to say?" Lanie asked, placing her hand over mine.

"Girl, it's my job to be the smartest, hottest, funniest, and most logical person in our little family." I pretended to give a hair flip.

"And you're so modest," Lanie added with a laugh. She leaned over and kissed my cheek. "Thank you."

"Thank you for the coffee. I'm going to run upstairs and look in on Angel. I'll be back down shortly."

TWENTY EIGHT

ANGEL

A FEW HOURS EARLIER

Waking up next to Marcus was the first time I felt safe in a man's arms after sex. Without moving, I noticed the clock on his side of the bed showed we'd slept for about six hours. I could feel his heart beating beneath my cheek, and the sound was soothing. He didn't snore, just lay there breathing softly.

As his chest slowly rose with each breath, I traced my fingers along his muscles feeling his strength while remembering how gentle he'd been with me, another thing I wasn't used to. I always assumed I only enjoyed rough sex, but after I'd experienced the opposite, I wanted more of that mixed in too. Watching him sleep, I was becoming more intimate than I'd ever been with someone. I could memorize the curves of his chest, admire the soft smattering of hair across his pecs, and gaze intently at the intricate tattoo on his right bicep instead of searching for the nearest exit as I usually did after sex. Reluctantly I moved away from him to give him space when he woke up.

He stirred slightly, rolling over onto his side to face me. Slowly his eyes opened and adjusted to his surroundings. "Good morning, beautiful."

"Not quite morning, middle of the night is more accurate." I knew his history was almost identical to mine and wondered if he was eager to flee. I didn't want him to feel trapped by staying here, but I also didn't want him to leave.

"I've never been someone to cuddle or sleep over, but—"

"You don't have to stay if you don't want to," I interjected saving myself from being disappointed when he asked to leave.

"As I was saying, I've never been someone to cuddle or sleep over, but all I want to do right now is feel you lying against me again. The last few hours were some of the best sleep I've had in a long time." I couldn't control the broad smile that formed on my face. At his request, I wrapped my arms around him and placed my head on his chest.

He combed his fingers through my hair and sighed. "I could get used to this quickly."

So could I. Already I'd given more of myself to this man than anyone before. We weren't just about sex; there were real feelings, and it felt even better than I could have ever imagined. I'd heard from

Gracie, Mary Jane, and Lanie about how amazing it was when you found that special guy, but I always blew it off as romantic drivel. I'd have gladly given them a chance to say I told you so at that moment. Without a doubt, no longer worried what might happen, I took a chance and said the thing I'd never said to anyone, "I've never been in love, so I'm not sure what it feels like, but if there's anything that feels better than this, I haven't experienced it."

Marcus's hand stopped moving. I peered up at him, and he asked, "What are you saying?"

"I'm saying I love you. And if you don't—"

His lips crashed against mine cutting me off from letting him have an easy out. After a few moments of a mind-blowing kiss, he said, "I love you. I was afraid to say it before, but after the way I felt waking up with you, I knew it was true. And I'm going to go ahead and tell you I want us to be exclusive. I don't want to share you with anyone."

"No one stands a chance with me after tonight, Marcus. I'm in this for the long haul. I've never said I love you to anyone but family or friends. It's not something I throw around lightly." My eyes drifted across the room as I spotted our reflection in the mirror on the back of my closet door. My caramel skin against his olive tone made for a beautiful combination. The eyes staring back at me in the mirror were unrecognizable though. They were no longer devoid of happiness, no longer filled with pain and bewilderment. I saw true joy, love, and even a bit of hope for what was to come. For once in my life, I liked the person I was seeing staring back at me.

"What are you thinking about?" Marcus's fingers grazed across my skin turning my face toward him.

"How happy I look. I barely recognize my own face in the mirror. My life over the past two years has been a crazy roller coaster full of flips and turns, and I've climbed mountains only to fall from them the moment I reached the top. I've been through hell, and I can finally see a light at the end of the tunnel." Tears filled my eyes with the revelation spilling forth.

Marcus should've run from the room as fast as possible. I was having a meltdown of epic proportions right in front of him, and he hadn't flinched. He was listening to me with concern, patiently waiting for me to finish talking instead of trying to change the subject or deflect the conversation to a less serious tone.

"When I thought of the future before, I couldn't see anything but a black hole. I had no idea where my life was going or who I'd be, even if I'd be alive in a couple of years. But now, I can see a future… with you. Does that scare the hell out of you?"

Marcus leaned forward and pressed his lips against mine, lingering there for a moment. "*Not* having a future with you is the only thing that scares the hell out of me." With those words, we cuddled back into the sleeping position and drifted off once more.

"Angel?" I heard my name whispered. Opening one eye I noticed the door was cracked open a bit. Cameron hadn't peered inside yet, so I covered Marcus's head and sat up.

"Cam? What's up?" At the sound of my voice, he popped inside and strolled to my side of the bed. The room was quite dark. I had blackout curtains, so he didn't seem to notice the other side of the bed was occupied.

"It's early afternoon. Lanie was worried you might be having a spell?" Cameron took up the small space left beside me on the bed and wrapped his arm around my shoulders. "Everything okay?"

"Yep. Just had a late night. What did you need?"

"I wanted to talk to you about Marcus. Did he tell you about his friend Calvin?" I knew Marcus had told Cameron about Calvin if I'd said no he would advise me to ask about him myself. Cameron was not only loyal, but kept a secret like no one else.

"Yes. Why?"

"Gavin and I want to take a trip to New York with Addy. We were hoping you and Marcus would want to go with us. You could help with Addy, and he could see his friend."

"Sounds like matchmaking to me. We've barely been on a few dates; don't you think it's too soon for us to take a vacation together?" I knew we'd professed our love a little while ago, but Cameron didn't. Marcus stirred a bit in the bed next to me, and Cameron shifted to look around me.

"What's the big sexy lump in your bed?"

"You think I'm sexy?" Marcus mumbled from beneath the covers.

Cameron flipped the lamp on next to my bed and grinned. "Too soon for a big vacation?"

Marcus sat up and rubbed his eyes. "What's this about a vacation?"

"New York, the four of us, and my daughter of course." He paused and raised his hand up to me. "First of all, a high five for your first overnighter." After smacking his hand, he pulled me into a hug. "I'm so happy for you two. I knew this would work out."

"I think I'll grab a shower and let you two talk." Marcus strutted over to the bathroom. Cameron and I both watched as his naked ass strolled away. He had no shame in his body, and no reason to have any.

"We said *it* last night," I told Cameron. He knew exactly what the *it* was I referred to, I could tell by the elation on his face.

"I'm happy for you, Angel-girl. So, about that vacation...." It didn't take much to convince me to say yes. Of course, he made me tell him everything he'd missed the night before. As I reached to grab a robe from the side of the bed, I noticed Cameron give himself a pat on the back.

When Marcus returned from the shower, he happily agreed to go out of town with us. The next step was for Cameron and Gavin to make the arrangements. "I'll take care of everything and call you both with the details."

TWENTY NINE

CAMERON

ONE MONTH LATER

Arriving in New York, we caught a cab to the hotel. I booked us a suite with two bedrooms. Once we were settled, Angel knocked on our bedroom door. "Marcus asked me to go see Calvin with him. So we're going to go now and meet up with you guys this evening for dinner?"

"Sounds good. We'll meet back here."

Addy had fallen asleep, so we were stuck in the room until her nap was over. With our gorgeous view of the city, I couldn't complain too much. I grabbed a couple of drinks from the minibar, and Gavin and I sat down on the balcony. "Our lives are so different from the last time we were here, the day of our wedding," I remarked, thinking about all the people in our lives now who weren't back then.

"You're right. Our family has grown leaps and bounds with adults and children. It's too bad we can't expand our own little family." Gavin stared off into the distance. Even without making eye contact, I could hear the hurt in his voice.

A year ago, at Christmas, Addy experienced her first snowfall, and Gavin and I decided to have another baby. For our second child, we wanted it to have Gavin's blood. We filled out the necessary paperwork, and they ran tests to determine the motility of his sperm. When they called us with the results, we were nervous and excited at the possibilities until we heard the results. Gavin was infertile. His heart was broken, but he said we could have a child with my DNA again. I said yes, at first. And then one day I overheard him on the phone with someone, and he was crying. He'd felt like a disappointment because he couldn't have children. I never considered how strongly it would affect him.

After hearing his confession to Derrick—I later discovered—I confronted him. I told him I'd never be disappointed in him, and Addy would be more than enough for us. The next few months were rough for us. Gavin had moments of depression where he wouldn't get out of bed. Eventually, he came to terms with it, but occasionally the subject still stung.

"Our family is perfect the way it is. When Addy wakes up, let's take her to see where we got married. I know she's too young to understand, but I'd still like to." We had a double wedding in Central Park with Gracie and Ashton. Two years later, Addy came into our lives.

"Maybe in a couple of years we can look into adopting again? Who says the kid needs to be blood related to either of us?" Gavin hadn't suggested adoption before, so I knew he'd made progress in dealing with his infertility. "My family isn't blood related, and I wouldn't trade them for anything in the world." To this day, I'd never met his biological parents, and based on the stories I'd heard of them, I had no desire to change that fact.

"You're right, but why wait a couple years? Let's look into it when we get home. I'm ready if you are." Gavin turned to face me with a smile on his face. With his hands against my cheeks, he pulled me in for a kiss.

"Let's wake our beautiful daughter up and go see this amazing city with her." Addy was awake playing with one of her toys when I walked in to get her. "Do you want to go to the park with your daddies, princess?"

"Yes!" she cheered, bouncing on the mattress.

We spent the first part of the day at Central Park. Afterward, we went to all the tourist spots we could make time for. By the end of the day, the three of us were ready for a nap, and we got back to the hotel with an hour to spare before Angel and Marcus returned.

THIRTY

ANGEL

"How long has it been since you've seen Calvin?" I asked Marcus. We'd hailed a cab outside the hotel, and he'd been quiet since the moment we got inside. At one point, I took his hand in mine and felt it tremble.

"Over two years. He moved to New York to pursue an acting career. His life was so busy we lost touch. We didn't speak until about six months ago when he called me up to tell me about his diagnosis."

"Are you nervous?" I knew the answer already. With our bodies sitting so close I could feel him trembling, and I squeezed his hand tighter.

"Mostly nervous about what he'll look like. I've seen movies with people in the late stages of the disease. I just wonder how accurate they are."

When we arrived at the house, he got his answer. Marcus rang the doorbell, and an older woman answered. "Marcus?" she croaked. She looked to be in her early seventies.

"You look as beautiful as ever, Mrs. Wilkins." Her cheeks filled with a rosy hue as he leaned over and gave her cheek a peck. "This is my girlfriend, Angel."

"Girlfriend? My, that's a first. And you chose well for your first, I must say. You're quite a beauty." Her white hair fell in curly wisps around her face and the rest was placed in a tight bun on the back of her head. Her eyes were tired with soft wrinkles at the sides. Her smile was warm and kind.

"Thank you, ma'am," I said with a smile. I wasn't sure who this woman was or how to respond to knowing I was the first person he'd called his girlfriend. I guess I should have expected it, since I'd never referred to anyone as a boyfriend before either.

"We came to see Calvin. Last I heard, he was living here. Are you visiting?"

She smiled sadly and shook her head. "I moved in last month to take care of him. He doesn't look like you remember, Marcus. My son is very weak." Now I knew she was Calvin's mother. She invited us inside, and we followed her to the kitchen where she offered us a cup of coffee. "Calvin's resting right now. If you have time to wait, you could make an old woman happy by spending some time with her."

Marcus reached for her hand and kissed the top of it. "You're not an old woman, Mrs. W. We'd love to spend time with you. We have a few hours before we're supposed to meet our friends again. Tell me about Calvin."

After taking a sip of coffee, she sighed and closed her eyes. "I always wanted him to settle down with a nice woman and have a family. I never liked him running from one woman to another, but never in a million years did I imagine it killing him. My biggest fear was to see him end up alone. Now I'd give anything for that to be his fate over this."

Marcus reached into his back pocket and pulled out his wallet. "My boss gave me a check for him. It will cover at least ten months of his meds. He said after that we can send more."

Mrs. Wilkins's eyes welled up with tears. "Sweetheart, it's so wonderful of you to want to help Calvin, but the meds are no longer working. We maxed out credit cards, mine and his, to pay for them, and the doctor said to stop because they weren't doing any good anymore. He's given him a few weeks at most. The hepatitis is what's killing him now, killing his liver quickly. All the meds he takes now are to keep him comfortable and out of pain." Watching Marcus's mouth drop open and seeing the fear in his eyes, I knew he hadn't expected the news to be so devastating. "And you should know his memory has faded a lot. It's much like dealing with dementia. He may not have any idea who you are when you go in there, Marcus. He hasn't forgotten me though, so if he remembers anyone else, I'd put my money on you."

He handed her the check from Cameron. "I still want you to have this. My boss… my friend… Cameron insisted on helping. Use this for his pain meds, and whatever is left, you can use to pay bills. If you need more, he said I just had to ask. His family is old money and he's got a huge heart so he loves helping people."

She patted his hand and accepted the check. "Thank him for me. Now, tell me about your beautiful lady here." Her attention turned to me, and I didn't know what to say. From what Marcus had told me not too long ago, this woman helped raise him with as much time as he spent at her house. I'd never met anyone's family before. "How did you two meet?"

"Funny enough, the same friend who gave me the check. Cameron and Angel have been friends for over a decade. He knew we'd get along well so he made sure we were thrown together more than once. Her past is a lot like mine, littered with regrets. Basically, we're perfect for each other." Hearing him lay out our relationship in that way was sort of sweet. To an outsider, it may not sound romantic. Living our lives the way we had, we knew we'd started something special.

"You two make a beautiful pair. I don't want to be presumptuous, but I know you and Calvin are a lot alike. Have you…" Her words trailed off, but we both knew what she wanted to ask.

"My tests came back negative. My second results came in just before we left on the trip."

"Thank God. I'm so thankful. I know my Calvin would be too." She checked her watch and said, "It's time for his next pain meds. Would you like to come in and see him now?" His eyes drifted over to me, the fear apparent in them. I reached out and took his hand as we followed her to the back bedroom.

The room smelled like a hospital, sterile but with the stench of sickness in the air. In the bed was a man who looked to be twenty years older than Marcus. His cheeks were sunken in, a grey tone to his skin. He was frail. His head turned toward the door as we walked in. With a tube across his nose, attached to a breathing machine, he opened his mouth, but his voice came out scratchy and low. Marcus squeezed my hand tightly. A tear fell from his eye. As he approached the bed, I spotted a photo on the nightstand. It was Marcus and a handsome, muscular guy who could give any of the Hemsworth brothers a run for sexiest man alive. It became too clear to me it was Calvin in the picture, but a far cry from the man in the bed in front of me.

"Marcus?" I smiled to know he remembered him. "Who's the babe?" he croaked, raising his finger and pointing toward me.

His whole demeanor changed from a heartbroken mess to poking jabs at a buddy. "That's my girlfriend, Angel. Don't be trying to use your smooth moves on her either. She's crazy about me so you'd just be wasting your time."

Calvin grinned and lifted his hand once more to wave at me. "Hi, Calvin, I've heard a lot about you." I linked my arm through Marcus's and tried to keep my composure. Though it seemed selfish to think about in that moment, I was grateful Marcus's test came back clean. I never wanted to see him in such pain.

"All lies," he struggled to say.

"Hey, man, let me do all the talking for a change, and you listen for once." Marcus used sarcasm to let Calvin know he didn't need to struggle. I didn't know how he could be so strong. In my mind, I pictured Cameron being in the situation, lying in the bed, and even the thought made me want to lose my mind.

"Came to say goodbye?" Calvin asked. Marcus cleared his throat. He waited a moment to speak, probably trying to swallow back the emotions.

"Yeah, man, I did. I tried to get here sooner, but the funds have been tight. A friend of mine bought the ticket for me so I could visit. I tried to be here a month or so ago, but the big storm kept me away." Mrs. Wilkins stepped next to the bed with a small paper cup with pills and a glass of water with a straw. The scene took me back to my days in rehab.

"It's okay," Calvin remarked after swallowing his meds. "You're here now." His sentences became more broken each time he tried to speak. "Look good."

"He won't be up much longer once the pills take effect. So make good use of your time. I'll leave you alone." Mrs. Wilkins stepped out of the room. I started to follow her, but Marcus grabbed my hand. When our eyes met, I saw the pleading in them for me to stay. In that moment, I knew my presence was helping him stay strong.

There was a chair in the corner of the room, so I moved it closer to the bed. Marcus insisted I sit in it when I offered it to him. My legs had been feeling weak, so I didn't argue. Calvin pointed at me and asked, "You okay?"

Not sure how, but he seemed to notice I was in pain. "I'm good, just a little muscle pain." Marcus's eyebrow furrowed, and I shook my head to hopefully let him know I didn't want a fuss made over me.

"Did you… get… tested?" he asked Marcus. I wanted so badly to be able to speak for him. His words sounded so strained I could only imagine the pain it caused him to spit them out.

"I did, twice. Both negative. I'm healthy." Marcus sounded almost guilty admitting it.

"Good." He patted his chest and said, "Can't tell, but I'm happy." A long low squeal sounded as Calvin gasped for air. Mrs. Wilkins popped her head in and said, "Don't worry. He's catching his breath, it happens occasionally. The machine will adjust. You're fine though, right, Cal?" He blinked and gave a slow nod.

When it seemed Marcus had gotten a little more comfortable with the situation, I stood up. "I'm going to give you two a little time alone. I want to visit with Mrs. W." I kissed Marcus's cheek, and he whispered a thank you before I left.

"Oh hello, dear," Mrs. Wilkins greeted me in the living room.

"Do you mind if I sit in here with you for a bit?"

"Of course not, I'd quite enjoy it. I'd love to get to know more about the woman who finally captured my sweet Marcus's heart. First off, tell me what is bothering you physically. I've seen the little cringes of pain in your face. I know it's probably terribly rude to ask, but I'm an old lady and decided I don't have enough time left to sit and wonder about things." Nothing she asked had offended me. I loved how open she was, especially when everyone around me had been on tiptoes since I went into rehab well over a year ago.

"I have multiple sclerosis. Marcus knows about it, but I've asked him not to make a fuss over me. It's a relatively new diagnosis so I'm learning to cope. It's nothing compared to what Calvin is going through."

"Thank God for that. I don't wish it on anyone." She paused a moment and handed me an album. "Care to see a few photos of Marcus and Calvin growing up?"

"I'd love to." As I looked through the photos, she told me the stories behind them. The two had definitely been a couple of ladies' men and had been jokesters as well. Apparently, according to Mrs. W, they loved to play pranks on anyone they knew. "Marcus has always been so handsome it seems."

"I wish you could have met my Calvin back then. He'd have charmed the pants off you. I suppose that talent is what got him here today." She paused, looked up at me, and then started laughing. I didn't know what to say. "Oh my, that was a terrible thing to say, wasn't it!" She continued. "I apologize. It's been so long since I laughed."

"Don't be sorry. I bet it would make Calvin happy to hear. It seems like his sense of humor would've appreciated the joke."

Patting my leg, she said, "I can see in your eyes how scared you are. Scared about your feelings for Marcus. You're wondering if he's through with his promiscuous lifestyle?"

"I've had my share of promiscuity as well. It goes a bit deeper. I'm not sure where we go from here, if I can be what he needs." After seeing Calvin, I knew our trip home could go one of two ways. Either Marcus would be overcome with guilt for being so healthy as his friend withered away or he'd grab onto life with both hands and live it to the fullest in honor of Calvin. Both situations scared me for different reasons. Being overcome with guilt would probably mean he'd end our relationship. As far as we'd come, I wasn't sure how'd I'd handle losing him. On the other hand, if he grabbed life by the balls, he'd probably want to push our relationship forward, maybe propose, and I wasn't sure I would be marriage material.

"You're doing a lot of heavy thinking over there. I can see it on your face. Why not tell me what's going on, and I'll see if I can help? I know I'm practically a stranger, but sometimes that's the best person to speak to." She was rather easy to talk to, and I could use advice from someone who knew Marcus for years. "Why don't you start by telling me what it is that you love about Marcus?"

"The first thing which comes to mind is his bravery. He saved our friend, Cameron, when he was attacked outside of their work. He's a loyal friend, very caring and trustworthy. And he's been so gentle with me. I'm not used to men treating me as though I could break." I'd been taking care of myself for years, but it was nice for someone else to want the job for a change.

She leaned closer and whispered, "He's not hard on the eyes either, is he, dear?"

I couldn't help but smile at the mischievous look on her face. "Definitely a looker. But he's so much more, too."

"Seems I misjudged you. You appear to be a lot surer of what you want than I thought. Anyone can see the love you feel for Marcus is strong. And I saw it in his eyes as well when he introduced you to me." She took a sip of tea and set the cup back down. "I'll let you in on a little secret. He and Calvin had a pact when they were younger. They'd never call anyone girlfriend and they'd never bring anyone home to meet either of their parents. What that means is, you're something rather special. And I saw the way Marcus looked at you when he introduced you to me. There wasn't just love in his eyes, but a sense of pride. In my opinion, the two of you have quite a future to look forward to for yourselves." No one knew the future for sure, I never believed in fortune-tellers or even fortune cookies, but somehow hearing Mrs. Wilkins say it, I felt a sense of relief come over me. Nothing about the feeling was logical, but life doesn't always make sense.

"Would you mind if I helped you clean up a bit? I know you

have your hands full with taking care of your son. Doing dishes is a specialty of mine." When we'd been in the kitchen before, I'd noticed the pile of dishes in the sink. I wanted to help her in some way and it was the only thing I could think of.

"I would love it. I can't stand when my house is a mess." Other than the kitchen, there was barely a thing out of place. I thought I had a lot on my plate until I came here and saw everything this woman did for her son.

I followed her into the kitchen. Filling up the sink with hot water, I started to soak the dishes. She stood beside me with a hand towel ready to dry and place them back in their rightful spot in the cabinets. "Marcus used to help me do dishes when he was younger. I never could get Calvin to do them, but he was an only child, so I admit he was spoiled." She paused, smiling, as she seemed to consider something for a moment. "I guess he never was an only child once Marcus came into our lives. They've been like brothers since the day they met."

"Marcus hasn't told me many stories about Calvin. I think it's hard for him to talk about now. But I do know he loves him very much. He was incredibly nervous about seeing him today." I finished the last dish and handed it over to be dried.

"He's gone back to sleep," Marcus said as he walked into the kitchen. "We had a good visit though. I made him let me do all the talking, which was a nice change."

Mrs. Wilkins's laughed. "Marcus barely got a word in edgewise around Calvin. That boy would talk to a wall. In fact, he'd prefer it because the wall wouldn't interrupt him!" Laughter filled the kitchen briefly. Passing by me, Marcus wrapped his arms tightly around his friend's mother. I could see the joy on her face as she held on to him. He brought a light back into her eyes from the moment she opened the door. I was glad the snowstorm had kept him away before because it allowed me to witness the moment.

"He looks pretty rough doesn't he, Marcus?" She wiped away the tears from her eyes as she sat down on a chair at the table.

"I knew what to expect, I'd done research, but it didn't prepare me for the reality as I hoped it would." He peered over at me and then to the sink. "You put Angel to work, I see."

"She volunteered. We had a little time to get to know one another, and you'd better hang on to her, Marcus. She's a keeper." I bit my lip and my eyes shifted to the ground. When I looked back up, Marcus stared back at me.

"I'm hanging on to her as tight as I can." My chest constricted. Seemed things would go the second way, grabbing life by the balls. He glanced at his phone. "As much as I hate to do this, we need to get going. We have to get back to the hotel to meet our friends."

I'd called for a cab and found there was one just a few minutes away. Mrs. Wilkins walked us to the door. She embraced me and whispered, "Don't be afraid. Things will work out exactly the way they're supposed to."

I wish I'd heard what she said when she hugged Marcus. Whatever it was, he smiled and gave her a nod before kissing her cheek. "I love you, Mrs. W. I'll keep in touch better now. I promise."

We waved goodbye as Marcus held the door for me to get in the backseat of the cab. He slid in next to me and held my hand for the duration of the ride back to the hotel. I didn't push him to speak so we sat in silence. After the day with Calvin, I was sure he'd had a lot to think about. We stepped out of the car at the hotel, and once we were alone in the elevator, he placed his arm around my waist and pulled me close to him. Our eyes met, and he said, "I love you," before our lips met in a tender kiss.

"I love you." And those were the only words spoken before we made it back to the suite. Gavin, Cameron, and Addy were sitting on the floor playing a game when we stepped inside.

THIRTY ONE

CAMERON

All of us were too tired to go out for dinner so we ordered room service instead. While waiting for it to be delivered, I asked Angel to help me with something in the bedroom. I wanted the details on what happened with Calvin.

"How did it go today?

"I don't know how Marcus handled it as well as he did. I saw pictures of Calvin from before and the man I met today was a shell of that man. They didn't look like the same person at all. I did get to talk to Calvin's mother though, and she was a breath of fresh air." Something was different between the two of them; I noticed it the moment they walked into the room a few moments ago.

"You two looked very chummy when you came back. Did you have a good talk about everything?"

"Actually, we barely spoke two words to each other throughout today. I mostly spoke to Mrs. Wilkins. But things between us are better than ever."

"How do you know if you didn't talk?" She'd lost me for a moment.

"Just a feeling between us. I don't know how else to describe it."

"I think I know the exact feeling you mean. I have it with Gavin quite often." Angel was about to get her happily ever after, and it was about damn time.

THIRTY TWO

ANGEL

TWO MONTHS LATER

Ever since we'd returned from New York, Marcus and I had barely left each other's side. I spent most nights at his house instead of mine. He had sent a present to Mrs. Wilkins after we got home, a laptop. Cameron offered to buy one for her, brand new with all the bells and whistles, but Marcus wanted to get it himself. He found a refurbished one online; the seller had great reviews for previous refurbs. He shipped it to her overnight. With it, he was able to talk to her about Calvin's illness and he had a few one-sided conversations with Calvin. In the beginning, Calvin said a few words here and there, but in the past few weeks, he'd lost the ability to speak.

We'd made plans to travel back to New York once more to see him, but the day before our flight was scheduled, Mrs. Wilkins called to tell us he'd passed away the night before. Marcus lay with his head in my lap the whole night. He wouldn't let me see the tears, but I knew they were there. I felt them on my lap and could see his body tremble. Eventually he fell asleep, most likely exhausted from the emotional day.

Late in the evening, he sat up and stretched. "Thanks for staying with me today. I know you wanted to be home tomorrow for Tristan and Lanie's closing." They were signing the paperwork on their new home, one I was supposed to live in as well. I'd gone with them to see it, and I was excited about my single apartment in the back. As excited as I was for them, nothing could pull me away from Marcus after the call about Calvin.

"They understood why I couldn't be there. They send their love too."

"Before we found out about Calvin, there was something I wanted to talk to you about. It may not be the best moment, but life's too short to wait, right?" Marcus took my hands in his, and I froze, sure this was a one-knee moment coming up. Instead, he said something I hadn't expected. "Instead of moving into the apartment at Tristan's, I hoped you might move in with me instead."

"Wow, I wasn't expecting that." I hoped he didn't notice how tense I'd become at first and how relaxed I was after he said it. I wasn't ready for a huge step like marriage, even though I couldn't imagine my life without Marcus in it.

"Well, what do you say? Will you move in with me?" he asked again.

"I'd love to." His apartment was smaller than I was used to with the three-bedroom house I was in now, but I'd spent so much time here lately it already felt like home. Lanie had already assured me they'd be fine without my help on the rent. "I'll tell them tomorrow. Tonight is all about you."

A few days later, I had packed up everything I owned and was sitting on my bed staring at an empty room. "Hello, beautiful. Are you ready to get this loaded into the van?" Gus asked. He stopped, probably noticing the terrified look on my face. Taking a seat next to me on the bed, he rested his hand on my shoulder. "What's up?"

"Are we moving too fast?"

"You've known each other almost a year now. I think it's a normal pace." Squeezing my shoulder, he said, "Remember rehab taught us to replace alcohol with something positive. Marcus is your something positive."

"I can't use him as an excuse not to drink. If I do and something happens, I'll have no reason left not to pick up a bottle."

"If that happened, then you'd use another lesson learned, how to reach out. You'd reach out to me and I'd convince you not to drink." His voice lowered. "Neither of us is going to end up like Mike. We'll never be cured of this disease, but we're going to fight it together, forever." Looking away from me momentarily, he added, "At least we don't have to fight it alone anymore." His eyes drifted up after a moment, and my mouth fell open when I saw a smile grace his lips.

"Who is she?"

"Remember the meeting we went to after your night with Marcus went so wrong?" I nodded. It was hard to forget the time in my life. It led me to every moment since then. "Karina, the girl speaking at the podium. We ran into each other at another meeting and started talking. We've been on a few dates."

I smacked his chest playfully and gasped, "You've been holding out on me!"

He laughed. "I didn't want to say anything until I was sure it was going somewhere. I really like her though, Angel."

I moved to sit on his lap and wrapped my arms around his neck. "Gus-Gus, I'm so happy for you."

"Should I be jealous?" Marcus's voice rang out, interrupting the moment.

"I'm the one who's jealous. You two have quite the life ahead of you. Maybe Karina will be my happily ever after. Time will tell, I suppose." Gus kissed my cheek, and the three of us loaded up the moving van with all the boxes. I turned to stare at the house I'd lived in for the past few years. The day was bittersweet. In a few weeks, Tristan and Lanie would be moved out, and none of us would come back here again. There were many memories within those walls, but I knew there were even more memories to be made in the years to come.

EPILOGUE

CAMERON

TWENTY-FIVE YEARS LATER

Christmas day tradition was for everyone to get together at one person's house. We rotated every year, and our family had outgrown all the houses. We began a new tradition. A Shot in the Dark was one of the hottest nightclubs in town, its success had grown higher than we'd ever expected when we first opened. During the CMA fest in town, some of the biggest names requested to play at our club. We'd expanded into the restaurant business because of it. Each restaurant was run by one of the families who originally began the club.

Looking around at each table, I smiled at how far we had come. Around thirty-five years ago, it started with just four of us, Angel, Gracie, Mary Jane, and me. Each of us had met our loves, expanded our family, and made it through every struggle life threw at us along the way.

Gracie and Ashton occupied a booth with their family. They were gushing over Autumn's engagement ring. Dalton had been her high school sweetheart. They'd graduated college together, begun their separate careers, and were ready to settle down. One thing was for sure, Autumn never had to suffer through Gracie's bad luck with men. She found her own Ashton with no problem.

Looking bored at the table was their fourteen-year-old son, Terrence, an oops baby who came along in Gracie's thirties. He was a good kid, top of his class, but he was a teenage boy who couldn't care less about engagement rings.

Gracie tapped Mary Jane on the shoulder and they began to gab away, probably planning the wedding already. Katelyn handed her newborn son to Derrick so she could get into the diaper bag. Her husband, Shane, chatted with Craig about sports. Craig was in the NFL. He'd gone to college on a full scholarship and had been scouted right after graduation. For four years, the group had cheered him on from our box seats. In his third year, the team almost made it to the Super Bowl. His boyfriend, Judd, helped Derrick entertain the baby. I approved wholeheartedly of him dating a Judd; if his last name had been Nelson, I'd have been more impressed.

Behind the bar, Tristan was loading up the dishes. "You can't help yourself, can you?" I asked. Tristan had been the head bartender for the first few years we were open. When we expanded, we offered him one of the restaurants to run, and he accepted.

"You know this place is my firstborn."

He went back to wiping the counter, and I stepped over to Lanie. "Everything okay with you? I saw the look just now."

"What you saw was a look of admiration. We heard back on the test results today. No sign of Alzheimer's. I'm so thankful. You have no idea how worried I've been. Each time he forgets where he put his phone or what he went into a room for I would worry."

"I forget why I go into a room most days," I teased. "But seriously, I'm so happy to hear it." Searching the room, I asked, "How's Loretta? Did she know about the testing?"

Their daughter, Loretta, named after his mom, was in college and had decided to be a doctor like her Aunt Macy. "She did. She held my hand while we waited on the results, and I didn't know how stressed she'd been until I watched her relax at the news. The three of us had a good cry of relief together."

Tristan walked up and placed his hand on my shoulder. "What are you guys whispering about over here?"

Saving Lanie from coming up with something, I asked, "When's your sister getting here?"

"Macy's doing an experimental brain surgery tonight. She sends her love to all of us. And she sent presents." He nodded in the direction of the tree where there was a pile of gifts in matching paper. "And my baby girl is over there with Gavin, Addison, and Evan."

Evan was the son we adopted. As soon as we returned from the trip with Angel and Marcus, we began the process. A year later, we had a baby boy. We chose the name Evan in honor of Mary Jane's maiden name. She'd done so much to help us achieve our dream of being parents, we wanted a chance to honor her for it. Addy loved having a baby brother. She used to tell us she wanted pretty chocolate skin like his. Evan was in college finishing up on a law degree.

My beautiful husband sat with our children and Loretta. Addison had pursued a career in fashion design. In my completely unbiased opinion, she was fabulous. Loretta was a few years younger, but they had become best friends and inseparable. The two of them along with Craig and Evan, reminded me a lot of the days when it was just Gracie, MJ, Angel, and me.

Angel sat in a booth across from Marcus. Her wheelchair was pushed behind the table. Ten years ago, her legs gave out from under her, and from that day on, she never was able to support herself standing up for more than a moment without pain. In the past few months, she'd been working with Macy. The hospital Macy worked for had a medical trial running for MS patients, and she was able to get Angel on the list. If the trial went well, she'd be back on her feet within a year or two. She married Marcus, and they had twin boys, who recently turned fifteen. They noticed how bored Terrence was and ran over to rescue him from the squealing women.

Angel had told Marcus she didn't want to have children because of her MS and alcoholism being enough to handle day-to-day. Together they made the decision not to ever try, but apparently, life had other plans for them. Angel had confided in me that she never saw herself as the mom type, but once those boys came along, it became the most natural thing in the world to her.

Mary Jane and Gracie moved over to sit with Angel while Marcus went to Ashton's table. Tristan joined the men, and the women waved me over. Just the four of us sitting together took me back to a time I loved but didn't want to return to. In the last twenty years plus our family had grown ten times, and I'd never been happier. I couldn't imagine my life without Tristan who was there for Mary Jane when she carried my baby girl. Or life without Marcus who put a smile on my Angel girl's face. Every person in this room had changed my life in some way.

"Cameron, you look far away there," Gracie said, waving her hand in front of my face.

"Just appreciating my big family here. I can't believe how much we've grown over the years. And we all still look so fabulous." I flicked my hand against my shoulder dusting off invisible lint.

"You're still so modest," Angel teased. "It seems like only yesterday we were hanging out at the club, complaining about men, and wondering where we'd be in twenty years." She looked around the room, the smile on her face growing larger each second. "I thought I'd be sitting alone watching the rest of you enjoy your happy marriages and all your children. I never thought I'd have a family of my own."

"The day I left for Disney, I never expected to see Derrick again. I thought for sure I'd be looking back on my life wondering what might have been." Mary Jane peered over at her husband and blew him a kiss when their eyes met.

"Let's not forget how I was convinced my Ashton was into guys. I almost lost the best thing that ever happened to me." She exchanged a cutesy look with her husband this time.

The three of them turned to face me and said, "And to think we owe it all to your meddling ways." I opened my mouth to argue, but Gracie stopped me. "We figured things out when you were having us help Marcus and Angel get together. Derrick told me what you did for him and MJ, and from there we put the other pieces together. The truth is, Cameron, you've known what the rest of us needed from the beginning. As many times as you've said it, we can more than agree, you're the best thing that's ever happened to any of us."

They raised their glasses, filled with nonalcholic bubbly, and said, "To Cameron, our fairy godfather." All of us burst into laughter as we clinked the flutes together in harmony.

THANK YOU

Thanks for reading *Twisted Fate* (The Southern Devotion series book 4). I do hope you enjoyed Angel and Cameron's stories. I appreciate your help in spreading the word, including telling a friend. Before you go, it would mean so much to me if you would take a few minutes to write a review and share how you feel about my story so others may find my work. Reviews really do help readers find books. Please leave a review on your favorite book site.

Don't miss out on new releases,
exclusive giveaways, and much more!

Newsletter: https://docs.google.com/forms/d/15zzqeS8owi_xjdd-fZdJUi0b1JY4wowXcBIwJ2deTn8

Facebook: www.facebook.com/AmyKMcclung

Facebook group: www.facebook.com/groups/McClungsminions

Twitter: www.twitter.com/AmythaMcclung

Pinterest: www.pinterest.com/amytha22

Goodreads: www.goodreads.com/author/show/6421342.Amy_K_McClung

Instagram: www.instagram.com/amykmcclung

I'd love to hear from you directly, too. Please feel free to e-mail me at amy.k.mcclung@att.net or check out my website www.amykmcclung.blogspot.com for updates.

ACKNOWLEDGMENTS

Writing the final story in this series was the hardest thing I've written so far. These characters were greatly inspired by some of the most important people in my life. Saying goodbye to them is like losing family. I want to thank my looza peeps for inspiring the idea for this series. The times we shared were some of the best in my life!

To Hot Tree Publishing, my gratitude is tremendous. You picked up this series and helped me shape and form it into an even better set of stories with amazing covers. I can't thank you enough for taking a chance on me and my writing. Besides the amazingly supportive Becky, Justine, and my fellow authors, you have the best editors and beta readers a girl can ask for. I've learned so much from this journey, and it's done nothing but improve my writing ability.

Many thanks to my mom who has read every story I've written and has promoted me more than anyone else. Gratitude to my dad who may not have read my books but always tells me how proud he is of me and raves about my books to anyone who will listen.

To all the readers who love this series, thank you for your support and kind words over the years. Thank you for loving these characters as much as I do. For laughing at their jokes, crying during their struggles, and cheering them on in their successes. Without your enjoyment of my work, there would be no purpose writing more.

Last but not least, thank you to Cameron, Gracie, Mary Jane, and Angel, the original cast of characters who began speaking to me one day and have kept me laughing over the last five years. My mind may have given you life, but your lives have taken me on a journey I never dreamed possible.

ABOUT THE PUBLISHER

Hot Tree Publishing opened its doors in 2015 with an aspiration to bring quality fiction to the world of readers. With the initial focus on romance and a wide spread of romance subgenres, we envision opening up to alternative genres in the near future.

Firmly seated in the industry as a leading editing provider to independent authors and small publishing houses, Hot Tree Publishing is the sister company to Hot Tree Editing, founded in 2012. Having established in-house editing and promotions, plus having a well-respected market presence, Hot Tree Publishing endeavors to be a leader in bringing quality stories to the world of readers.

Interested in discovering more amazing reads brought to you by Hot Tree Publishing? Head over to the website for information:

www.hottreepublishing.com